IF
ONLY
IT
WERE
TRUE

IF ONLY IT WERE TRUE

MARC LEVY

FOURTH ESTATE • London

First published in Great Britain in 2000 by
Fourth Estate Limited
6 Salem Road
London W2 4BU
www.4thestate.co.uk

10 9 8 7 6 5 4 3 2 1

Printed in Great Britain by Mackays of Chatham plc

For Louis

PART
ONE

JUNE

One

THE NOVELTY CLOCK SITTING ON THE UNPAINTED WOODEN nightstand sounded at five-thirty. Curled under a light down comforter in the middle of her large iron bed, Lauren opened her eyes to the clear golden light of dawn unique to a rare nonfoggy San Francisco summer morning.

Half-asleep, she fumbled for the button to turn off the alarm. She rubbed her eyes and looked down at her dog, Kali, who sat up eagerly, expectantly, on the heavy-knit rug beside her.

"Don't look at me like that, I don't even feel human yet!"

At the sound of her voice, the dog leaped onto the bed and rested her head on her owner's belly. Lauren stroked her and yawned. Then she remembered what day it was. "Move, sweetie! I have to get up and make us both some breakfast."

It had been another too short night's rest. Lauren was a resident at San Francisco Memorial Hospital, and yesterday's tour of duty had lasted well beyond the usual twenty-four hours because of a last-minute influx of burn victims from a major fire. The first ambulances had roared into the emergency entrance ten minutes before she was due to finish. Without waiting for the relief team, Lauren began evaluating the injured. With the swift, practiced moves of an experienced emergency-room doctor, she checked the vital signs of each patient, stuck a colored label on each chart indicating the seriousness of the victim's condition, assigned a preliminary diagnosis, gave orders for the first lab tests, and directed the orderlies to the appropriate areas. Screening the sixteen victims was complete by 12:30 A.M., and at a quarter to one, the surgeons, recalled for the emergency, began the first operations of this long night.

Lauren had assisted her supervisor, Dr. Fernstein, through two successive operations. She had not left until well after two, when Fernstein ordered her home, warning her that if fatigue got the better of her vigilance, she could be putting the lives of her patients in danger.

She had driven through the deserted city streets at the wheel of her now antique Triumph Herald convertible. "I'm too tired and I'm driving too fast," she had repeated to herself like a mantra, fighting the urge to sleep. Every time she left the hospital this late, she reminded herself that she had to get the Triumph fitted with seat belts. The idea of returning to the emergency room under the spotlights, rather than backstage, was enough to keep her awake.

She activated the remote control to the garage door and parked the old car. Taking the inside hallway, she climbed the stairs four at a time, relieved to be home. Blearily entering her apartment, she headed toward the kitchen to make some herbal tea. The jars brightening the shelf held every type and flavor, as though there were a special aroma for each moment of the day. In her bedroom she set her cup on the nightstand, dropped her clothes to the floor, climbed into bed, and almost immediately fell asleep.

The day just past had been much too long, and the day soon to begin required an early start. Taking advantage of two days off, which for once coincided with the weekend, she had accepted an invitation to stay with friends in Carmel. Although her accumulated fatigue certainly justified sleeping in, nothing was going to make her waste the rare beauty of an early-morning drive down Route 1. Lauren loved the Pacific Coast Highway between San Francisco and Monterey, loved seeing the sun crest the high coastal hills and sparkle on the cold Pacific below.

Lauren stretched her arms and legs, yawned enormously, jumped out of bed, and shrugged into the big cotton T-shirt hanging on the bedpost. Kali at her heels, she went into the living room, stopping briefly to enjoy the warm shaft of sunlight streaming through the window. Lauren reveled in the cozy charm of her apartment. Set on the top floor of a well-kept Victorian house on Green Street, it had a small kitchen-dining area; a living room complete with fireplace, leaded cabinets, and intact period detail; a spacious bedroom; and a vast bathroom with a walk-in closet and a window overlooking the Bay set just over the bathtub. The bathroom floor was painted white with a black-stenciled-checkerboard pattern Lauren had designed herself. The living room's white walls sported old drawings of San Francisco Lauren had hunted down in the galleries on Union Street. The ceiling was edged with a hand-carved, turn-of-the-century wooden molding, refinished to a pristine golden oak that matched the built-in cabinetry. She had furnished the room with a big inviting couch upholstered in off-white raw cotton, and fawn-colored Oriental rugs. She was proud of her apartment; it was the first home that had ever been truly hers—purchased with the inheritance her father, who had died when she was still a toddler, had left her. She knew that her father would have loved this place, loved to watch the sailboats in the Bay, whereas sometimes she felt her mother only loved the idea that her daughter might at last be settling down. Ha, she wished! Lauren's schedule in the past two years hadn't much improved since her internship's slave hours, but she had devoted her few moments of leisure to decorating her apartment, to make it feel like her own.

She moved into the small kitchen and got Kali her breakfast, IAMS special served in a heavy earthenware dish.

Then she assembled butter, strawberry jam, an English muffin, a bowl of cereal, a container of peach yogurt, half a grapefruit, and a cup of coffee on a tray. Kali watched her, cocking her head inquisitively. "Yes, I know—but I'm hungry!" Lauren sternly pointed Kali's head back to her food dish and took her own tray to her desk in the living room. From the window, if she tilted her head a little, she could see the Golden Gate Bridge stretching elegantly between the two points of the Bay, and beyond it, the houses clinging to the hills of Sausalito and the fishing port of Tiburon. Directly below her, roofs descended like steps toward the Marina. She opened the window wide: the city was still sleeping; the only sounds relieving the morning languor were the mewing of gulls and the low horns of the big freighters, moaning as they shipped out for the Orient. She stretched again, then tucked into her breakfast with a hearty appetite. Three times last night she had tried to take a bite of her sandwich, but each time her beeper had squealed its shrill summons to a fresh emergency. When people met her and asked what it was like to work in an ER, expecting her to expound upon profound issues of life and death, Lauren invariably told them, "I don't have time to ponder profound issues of life and death. There's not even time to eat."

Now, at last, she had a weekend with no crisis to be faced, and she could just *be*. Having polished off the better part of her feast, she took her tray to the sink and went to the bathroom. She slid her fingers between the wooden slats of her blinds to work them shut, let her cotton T-shirt fall to the floor, and stepped into the shower. The warm, powerful jets finished the waking up process.

Wrapping a towel around her, she made a face in the mirror. Her skin was pale, despite its being summer, but she still decided against makeup for the day. She threw on a pair of jeans and a polo shirt, took off the jeans and put on a skirt, took off the skirt and pulled the jeans back on. She took a canvas bag from the closet and stuffed in a toilet kit, a bathing suit, and a few changes of clothing. Then she tied a big red scarf around her hair so that the drive in the convertible wouldn't render it a hopeless, tangled mess. Voilà! She now felt ready for her weekend.

Walking back through her apartment, she noticed the extent of the disorder—clothes on the floor, towels everywhere, dishes in the sink, bed unmade—assumed a decisive air, and said aloud to all her household objects, "Not a word, no grumbling! I'll be back tomorrow evening to straighten you all up for the week!"

Then she took a pencil and paper and wrote a note, which she stuck to the refrigerator door with a large frog magnet:

Mom

Don't dare clean up, I'll take care of it when I get back.

Thanks for looking after Kali. I'll pick her up from your place Sunday around five.

Love you. Your favorite physician

She slipped on her coat and leaned down to tenderly pat her already whining dog. "Sorry, Kali. I need a break. Be good!" She planted a kiss on Kali's forehead, rose, and left the apartment, taking the outside stairs to the garage, and almost made it into her aging convertible with one jump.

"I'm off, I'm really off!" she said exultantly. "It's a miracle. Although now of course we have to pray that you'll agree to start. If you cough just one time, I'll drown your engine in maple syrup and turn you over to the junkyard. Then I'll replace you with a snazzy new model, fully loaded, that doesn't throw tantrums if it's cold in the morning. Got that straight? Let's go!"

The old English lady must have been impressed by the ring of conviction in her mistress's voice, for her engine came alive on the first twist of the key. A beautiful day had begun.

Two

Lauren eased the Triumph onto the street quietly, not wanting to awaken her neighbors. As soon as she reached the next block, she tuned her radio to 101.3 FM and turned up the volume. As the car sped through the empty streets, the pale morning light became brighter, polishing the dazzling perspective of the city. Lauren loved the thrill of climbing up and down the steep hills of San Francisco, loved the slight vertigo the downward plunge always brought to her stomach.

As she made a tight left onto Stockton Street, she heard an odd noise, a rattling, perhaps from the transmission. Probably nothing, she thought as she zoomed down the steep slope toward Union Square. It was six-thirty, Bruce Springsteen was celebrating with "Glory Days" on the radio, and Lauren felt happy, happier than she had been for a long time. Bye-bye, stress; bye-bye, hospital. She sang along with Bruce, at one with the spirit of the song. Union

Square was quiet. In a few hours the sidewalks would be spilling over with tourists and locals, shopping in the department stores around the square. The cable cars would file one after the other, shop windows would light up, and a long line of cars would form at the entrance to the central underground parking garage. Above it, in the gardens of Union Square, bands of musicians would gather to trade notes and songs for a few cents.

But now, on this early weekend morning, the storefronts were darkened, the gates still pulled over the display windows. A few homeless people were still sleeping on benches, and the parking lot attendant dozed in his booth at the entrance to the underground garage. The Triumph was sailing; the lights were green all the way. Lauren felt exhilarated as the fresh morning air enlivened her senses, billowed over her head scarf. She shifted down to second as she approached her turn onto Geary in front of Macy's vast facade. Perfect cornering, a soft squeal of tires, then a strange noise, a series of clicks. Everything was moving fast. The clicking became a blur of metallic sounds.

A sudden bang! Time stopped. All dialogue ceased between the steering and the wheels. The car swerved sideways and skidded on the damp surface. Lauren's hands gripped the useless steering wheel. It offered no resistance, spinning in a limbo of its own. The car continued to skid; the seconds passed in infinitely slow motion. Lauren felt her head spin, although in reality it was the scene around her that was spinning at an astonishing speed. The Triumph turned like a top on the slick asphalt until the wheels slammed into the curb. The front end skidded into the air and was stopped only by a fire hydrant's catching on the undercarriage as if in an embrace. The hood lunged toward the sky. In one last effort, the car rotated on its axis and ejected its driver, by now much too heavy for the gravity-defying pirouette.

Lauren's body was hurled into the air, falling back down to crash against Macy's facade. The huge window exploded. Lauren lay in the blanket of glass, her hair tangled amid the debris. The old Triumph completed its long career lying on its back, half on the sidewalk. A plume of steam rose from its entrails, and then it breathed its ladylike last. Lauren lay still, peaceful, at rest. Her features were calm, her breathing slow and even. There might even have been a small smile on her slightly parted lips. Her eyes were closed—she seemed to be sleeping. Her long hair framed her face, her right hand lay across her midriff.

The parking lot attendant in his booth blinked hard. He had been aroused by the sound of the impact, had witnessed everything. "Just like in the movies, only this time it was for real," he would later say. He rose, ran outside, then changed his mind. He clawed frantically for the phone and dialed 911.

Within ten minutes the San Francisco Memorial Hospital EMS arrived. Two policemen were already on the scene. Dr. Philip Stern, the resident on duty, ran over to Lauren's body lying on the sidewalk and yelled to his colleague to come quickly. Using scissors, he cut through jeans and T-shirt.

"Let's get an EKG and start an IV. I've got a thready pulse and no pressure, respiration forty-eight, cut on head, looks like a closed fracture of the left femur with internal hemorrhage. Get me two units."

Stern's partner Frank, the EMS paramedic, pasted electrodes on the young woman's chest, connecting each one with a different-colored wire to the portable electrocardiograph. He switched it on, and the screen instantly leapt to life.

"What's it show?" asked Philip.

"Nothing good; she's going. Pressure, eighty over sixty; pulse, a hundred and forty; lips are blue.

"Give me a number seven endotracheal tube. I need to intubate."

The paramedic finished placing the IV catheter in Lauren's arm and handed the bag of saline to one of the policemen.

"Hold that good and high, I need both hands."

Lauren's temperature began to fall rapidly, while the tracing on the EKG grew erratic. At the bottom of the green screen, a small red heart began to blink, followed at once by a short repeated beep, a warning that heart failure was imminent.

In under a minute, they had secured an airway. Stern asked for a report on her vital signs, and Frank replied that respiration was still stable but pressure had fallen to fifty. He had no time to finish his sentence: the short beep was replaced by a shrill alarm from the machine.

"That's it, she's in V-fib. Give me three hundred joules."

Philip picked up the two paddles of the apparatus and rubbed them together.

"Go ahead, you have the juice," yelled Frank.

"Pull back, I'm hitting her."

Under the jolt of the discharge, the body arched brutally before falling back.

"Nope, no good."

"Try three-sixty, let's go!"

"Three-sixty it is, go ahead!"

"Pull back!"

The body again rose and fell back lifelessly. "Give me

another five of epinephrine and reload to three-sixty. Pull back!" Another jolt, another spasmodic leap. "Still fibrillating! We're losing her: inject one unit of lidocaine into the IV and reload. Pull back!" The body heaved upward. "Give her an amp of bicarb and reload to three-eighty *stat!*"

With the new shock, Lauren's heart seemed to be responding to the injected drugs and had returned to a normal rhythm, but not for long. The alarm signal, which had briefly ceased, shrilled out louder than ever. "Cardiac arrest!" exclaimed Frank.

Immediately, Philip began a cardiac massage with extraordinary determination. As he worked to bring her back to life, he was begging, "Don't do this to us. It's a fine day today. Don't be stupid. Come back!" He told his partner to reload the machine.

Frank tried to calm him down. "Let her go, Philip, it's no good."

But Stern would not give up; he again yelled at Frank to reload the defibrillator, and his partner complied. Yet again Philip shouted, "Pull back!" and once more the body arched. But the electrocardiogram remained stubbornly flat. Philip went back to cardiac massage, his forehead beaded with sweat. His partner realized that Philip had lost his sense of reality. He should have stopped trying and pronounced the time of her death. But nothing could stop him. He went on massaging Lauren's heart.

"Give another shot of epinephrine and go up to four hundred joules."

"Philip, stop, this makes no sense. She's dead. You don't know what you're doing."

"Shut up! Do it!"

The policeman looked questioningly at the doctor kneeling beside Lauren, but Philip was focusing on his patient. Frank shrugged, injected another dose into the IV tubing and reloaded the defibrillator. He called out the threshold level of four hundred joules, and Stern delivered it, without even asking to pull back. Jolted by the current, the torso jerked violently upward. The EKG remained hopelessly flat-line. The resident did not look at it. He pounded his fist on Lauren's chest. "Damn! Damn!"

Frank grabbed him by the shoulders and shook him. "Come back to me, buddy."

Spellbound, the policemen watched the two. Philip, crumpled and on his knees, slowly raised his head and said in a low voice, "Time of death: seven-ten."

Frank turned to the policeman who was still awkwardly holding the IV bag and said, "It's over. There's nothing more we can do." Frank rose, laid his arm across his partner's shoulder, and walked him toward the ambulance. Then Frank came back to the police officer and asked, "Could you please take care of the body. We are well over our time of duty, and to be honest I'd rather not have my buddy go on longer with this nightmare. He took it really bad."

The policeman nodded. "You're lucky we have a van today. Go and rest, you deserve it."

Thanking him with a wave of his hand, Frank turned back to Philip, who was waiting, already fastened to his passenger seat. "Come on, we're off."

While the ambulance disappeared around the corner, the two policemen lifted Lauren's inert body. They set it on the stretcher, covered it with a blanket, then placed it in the back of the police van.

Inside the EMU the two medics had not said a word.

Frank broke the silence. "What got into you, Philip?"

"She's not even thirty years old . . . her whole life ahead of her . . . she's drop-dead beautiful."

"Yes, and that's just what she did! It's fate; you can't do a thing about it. It was her time. When we get back, put all this shit behind you and forget about it."

Meanwhile, two blocks behind them, the police van was entering an intersection when a convertible Saab raced through the light as it changed. Furious, the policeman braked sharply and sounded his horn, while the driver babbled his apologies. The sudden stop hurled Lauren's body off the stretcher. The two men went to the rear, the younger one taking Lauren's ankles, the older one taking her arms. His expression froze when he looked at the young woman's chest.

"She's fuckin' breathing!"

"What?"

"She's breathing, I tell you. Get behind the wheel. Move it. We've got to get to the hospital."

The police van caught up with the ambulance. As it roared past them, the two puzzled medics recognized "their" cops.

"Why were they driving that way?"

"Who knows?" said Frank. "Maybe it wasn't them. They all look alike."

Ten minutes later they pulled up at the ER entrance alongside the police van, whose doors were still open.

Philip went into the hospital and hurried toward the ER check-in desk. Skipping any preliminary greeting, he blurted out, "Did they just bring someone in?" Not waiting for a reply, he insisted, "Where is she?"

"The woman in the car accident?" asked the receptionist. "Area three. Fernstein's with her. Apparently she's one of his team."

Behind him, the older policeman tapped him on the shoulder. "What shit were you medics playing at?"

"I beg your pardon?"

How was it he had pronounced a young woman dead when she was still breathing in his van? "You realize that if I hadn't noticed, we'd have put her into cold storage alive? You haven't heard the last of this."

At that moment, Dr. Fernstein emerged from area three. Seeming not to notice the officer, he spoke directly to the young doctor. "Stern, how many doses of epinephrine did you give her?"

"Five milligrams, four times."

The professor at once reprimanded Philip for administering intensive resuscitation measures when the case did not warrant them. Then, turning to the police officer, Fernstein said that Lauren was dead well before Dr. Stern announced the time of death.

Fernstein added that the EMS team's only mistake was in its overzealous attempts to revive the heart, at taxpayers' expense. Concerning what had happened next, he explained that the accumulation of drugs they'd injected had pooled around the pericardium. "When you slammed on the brakes, the medication flowed into her heart, which reacted to the chemicals and started to beat again. Unfortunately, that did not alter that the victim was brain-dead. As for her heart, as soon as the cardiac drugs wore off, it would again stop, if it hasn't already done so." Fernstein suggested that the officer apologize to Dr. Stern for his totally inappropriate comments, then asked Stern to come and see him.

The older cop turned to Philip and mumbled, "I see the police aren't the only ones to close ranks and protect their own." The cop turned on his heel and left the hospital building. Even though the double doors of the emergency bay were closed, you could hear the slam as he shut the van doors.

Stern remained standing with his arms on the reception desk. He looked at the nurse, squinting. "What the hell's this all about?" The duty nurse shrugged and reminded him that Dr. Fernstein was waiting.

Philip knocked at the half-open door to the office of Lauren's boss. "Come in," said Fernstein. Standing behind his desk, his back turned to Stern as he gazed out the window, he was obviously waiting for Stern to speak first. Philip admitted that he was puzzled by what the professor had told the policeman.

Fernstein interrupted him coldly. "Listen, Stern. That policeman was upset. I offered him an explanation to set his mind at ease, and to keep him from filing a report that might ruin your career. Your handling of that resuscitation was unacceptable for someone of your experience."

"But how do you explain that she started breathing again?"

"I can't explain it and I don't have to. She's dead, Dr. Stern. You may not like it, but she's gone. I don't give a damn if her lungs are moving and her heart is beating on its own, her electroencephalograph is flat. We'll let things take their course and then send her down to the morgue. Period."

"But you can't do that. Not with so much evidence to the contrary! You've got to try something!"

Fernstein shook his head and raised his voice. He did not need to be told what he could or couldn't do. Did Stern know how much one day of intensive care cost? He ordered Stern to get out of his sight. The young doctor stood his ground, restating his argument with renewed vigor. When he had declared Lauren dead, his patient had been in cardiorespiratory arrest for several minutes. Her heart and lungs had stopped functioning. Yes, he had kept trying to bring her back, because for the first time in his life as a doctor he had felt that this woman did not want to die. He told Fernstein that her eyes had remained open, and he sensed her struggling, refusing to go under, and a few minutes later, defying all logic, and everything he had learned, her heart had started beating and her lungs had begun to inhale and exhale again—the breath of life. He begged Fernstein not to give up on her. In some cases people had inexplicably emerged from coma after six months or more. The way she had come back to life was already miraculous. So who cared how much it would cost? "Don't let her go, she doesn't want to, that's what she's telling us."

After a moment's silence, Fernstein replied, "This conversation is over."

Stern left the office without closing the door. A few seconds later, Dr. Fernstein picked up the phone, hesitated, put it down, took a couple of steps to the window, then grabbed the phone again. He asked for the surgical suite and was immediately connected.

"Fernstein speaking. Get ready. I need a neurosurgeon. We're operating in ten minutes. I'll send up the chart."

He replaced the phone carefully, and left his office.

Fernstein entered the operating room in a close-fitting, green scrub suit. A nurse pulled his sterile gloves over his hands; the surgical team already surrounded Lauren's body. Behind her head, a monitor displayed the rhythm of her breathing and heartbeat.

"How are her vital signs?" Fernstein asked the anesthetist.

"Stable, unbelievably stable. Sixty-five and one-twenty

over eighty. Her blood gases are normal. She's asleep, you can begin."

Calling them "my dear colleagues," Fernstein explained that they were about to see a professor of surgery with twenty years' experience perform an operation worthy of the skills of a second-year resident—setting a fractured femur.

"And do you know why I'm doing it? Because no self-respecting resident would perform such an operation on a patient who had been brain-dead for more than two hours." He added that he would therefore appreciate it if nobody asked him any questions. Setting the broken leg would take fifteen minutes at most. He thanked them for going along with him on this one.

Lauren was one of his students. All the medical staff present in this room knew how hard this must be for the surgeon and were determined to go through it with him. A radiologist came in and mounted a CT scan on the viewbox. The images showed a bloodclot on the brain. To relieve the pressure, a hole was drilled in the back of Lauren's skull and a fine needle passed through the meninges, controlled by a screen and directed by the neurosurgeon to the site of the hematoma. The brain itself appeared unharmed. Fluid began to drain through the tubing. Almost instantly the intracranial pressure dropped. The anesthetist adjusted the respirator to increase the flow of oxygen to the brain. Once decompressed, the brain cells reverted to a normal metabolism, gradually eliminating the accumulated toxins. Minute by minute, the nature of the endeavor was changing. The whole team gradually forgot that they were operating on a person who was clinically dead. Everyone entered into the spirit of the task at hand, one skilled move following another, in a swift and efficient series. Two hours later, Dr. Fernstein snapped his gloves off. He asked the team to close the incisions and transfer his patient to the recovery room. He ordered the nurses to take Lauren off the respirator once the anesthesia had worn off.

Once again he thanked the team for their help and their future discretion. Before leaving the OR he asked one of the nurses, Betty, to let him know when she disconnected Lauren. Leaving the suite, he walked quickly toward the elevators. Lauren was taken from the OR to the recovery room. Betty connected the cardiac monitor, the electroencephalograph, and the respirator. Thus arrayed, the young woman lying on the bed looked like an astronaut. The nurse took a blood sample and left the room. The sleeping patient looked peaceful; her eyelids seemed to trace the contours of a soft, deep universe of sleep. Half an hour went by, and Betty called Dr. Fernstein to say that Lauren had come out from the anesthesia and that her vital signs were stable. Betty wanted to be sure about the next step: she asked Dr. Fernstein to confirm his previous order.

"Disconnect the respirator. I'll be down in a while."

Betty went back into the room. She detached Lauren's breathing tube from the extension tubing leading to the machine, allowing her patient to try to breathe on her own. A few moments later she pulled out the tube altogether, freeing Lauren's throat. She brushed a strand of Lauren's hair back from her forehead, smiled tenderly at her, and went out, turning the light off behind her. Now the room was bathed in the faint green glow from the encephalograph. The line was still flat.

At the end of the first hour, the EEG tracing began to wobble, very slightly at first. Suddenly, the needle jerked upward to delineate a sharp peak, then fell sharply downward before returning to the horizontal.

As fate would have it, no one witnessed this anomaly. An hour later Betty returned to the room. After taking Lauren's vital signs, she unrolled a few inches of the telltale strip of paper the machine had generated. Betty noticed the strange peak, frowned, and read a few inches more. Since the rest of the tracing was flat-line, she threw the strip in the trash without wondering further. She took the phone off the wall and called Fernstein.

"It's me. We have a deep coma with vital signs stable. What do I do?"

"Find a bed on the fifth floor, and thanks, Betty."

Betty feared the worst—that although Lauren's vital signs were stable, only her primitive brain stem was still functioning. Her cortical function, the function that made her Lauren, made her see, feel, and act, made her a living human being, seemed to be completely gone.

PART TWO

NOVEMBER

Three

ARTHUR OPENED THE DOOR TO THE STREET-LEVEL garage with his remote control and parked his Saab. He climbed the outside staircase that led from the garage to his new third-floor apartment, swung the door shut with his foot, put his briefcase down, took off his coat, and collapsed onto the couch. Several cardboard boxes were still stacked in the living room, waiting to be unpacked. He had moved in only ten days ago, and he hadn't brought much with him—only his draftsman's table, his work files, his CDs, and his art and architecture books. Only after his relationship with Carol Ann had finally, definitively fallen apart had he accepted that it was time for him to move on, to try to start living his own life again, rather than the somewhat tentative, temporary one he'd grafted onto hers.

He'd been lucky to find this apartment. An architect specializing in the restoration of homes, he was amazed by how comfortable he'd immediately felt when he'd entered this apartment. Whoever had designed this environment had a keen sense of life and had created a home of taste and charm—and coming from Arthur, that was a supreme compliment. He hadn't had to change anything—just fit his draftsman's table between the fireplace and the writing desk, buy some towels and linens and rudimentary kitchen supplies, and he'd had an instant home.

He changed his suit for a pair of jeans and began to unpack his books and CDs, arranging them alphabetically on the shelf by the fireplace. When he had finished, he stood back and contemplated his perfectly ordered collections. "I think I might be getting a bit obsessive," he said to himself.

He went to the bathroom, hesitated between a shower and a bath, finally opting for the bath. He started the water running, switched on the little radio sitting on the radiator next to the walk-in linen closet, undressed, and sank into the tub with a sigh.

As Peggy Lee sang "Fever" on 101.3 FM, Arthur dunked his head several times under the water. There was something odd about the acoustic quality of the song. He was surprised by the stereo effect, particularly since his radio had only one, crummy internal speaker. He sat up straight in the bath and listened carefully. It sounded as though the finger-snapping accompanying the tune came straight from the linen closet. Intrigued, he emerged from the water and crept over to investigate. The sound was becoming more and more distinct. He paused, took a deep breath, and abruptly threw open the doors. His eyes widened, and he stumbled back.

Huddled on the floor beneath the hangers sat a young woman, eyes closed, seemingly transported by the rhythm of the song, humming along and snapping her fingers.

"What are you doing here?" he asked, shocked, and amazed, all at once. "Who are you?"

The woman jumped and looked at him with wide, startled eyes. "You can see me?"

"Of course I can see you."

She seemed astonished that he should be looking at her. "You can hear me?"

He pointed out that he wasn't blind or deaf and asked again, "What are you doing here?"

"This is wonderful, amazing!"

Arthur saw nothing "wonderful" about the situation, although there was plenty that was "amazing." Increasingly irritated, he asked, "What, I repeat, are you doing in my bathroom closet?"

"I don't think you realize. Touch my arm."

He stood there nonplussed as she held out her arm.

"Please . . ."

"No, I won't touch your arm. What's going on here?"

She took Arthur's wrist and asked him if he felt it when she touched him. Greatly exasperated, he confirmed that he did indeed feel her touch, that he saw her, and that he heard her perfectly well. For the fourth time, he asked her who she was and what she was doing in his bathroom closet.

She ignored his question. "I just can't believe it. You can actually see me, hear me, and feel me. This is fabulous."

Arthur was in no mood for this game. "Okay, that's enough! What is this, a practical joke? A call girl from my partner as a housewarming gift?"

"Are you always this rude? Do I look like some sort of hooker?"

Arthur sighed. "No, you don't. You're just hiding in my closet in the middle of the night."

"And yet you're the one who's naked, not me."

Arthur, startled, grabbed a towel and wrapped it around his waist as he tried to compose himself.

"All right now, the joke is over, you can come out of there, go home, and tell Paul it was lame. Very, very lame."

She did not know Paul, she told him. "And could you please stop yelling. Other people may not be able to hear me, but I can hear perfectly well."

Arthur was much too tired for this nonsense, and he wasn't going to play twenty questions trying to figure out what was really going on.

"Listen," he told the young woman before him, "it seems you're quite disturbed, but it's not my problem. I've just finished unpacking, and I'm very tired and I really need some peace and quiet. Please, please stop whatever game you're playing and go home. And come out of that closet, for God's sake!"

The young woman looked at him sadly. "I'm afraid it's not that easy. I haven't quite gotten the knack yet, though it's gotten better the last few days."

"What's 'gotten better' the last few days?"

"Shut your eyes, I'm going to try."

"To try what?"

"To get out of this closet. That's what you want, isn't it? So shut your eyes, I have to concentrate. And don't say anything for a couple of minutes."

"This is completely insane!"

"Oh, please. Just shut up and close your eyes. Then we won't have to spend the night here."

Not knowing what else to do, Arthur obeyed. Two seconds later he heard a voice coming from the living room.

"Not bad. I just missed the couch, but still, not bad at all."

He hurried from the bathroom and saw the young woman sitting on the floor in the middle of the room. She acted as though nothing were out of the ordinary.

"I'm glad you've kept the rugs, but I can't stand that painting on the wall," she said, indicating his college attempt at abstract expressionism.

"I'll hang whatever painting I want, wherever I want. I don't know how you do this place-shifting business. And really, I don't care. I simply want to go to bed. So if you won't tell me who you are, fine. I don't need to know. I beg you, just go home!"

"I am home! Or at least, I was. It's all so confusing."

Arthur shook his head. "Listen, I moved in here ten days ago. This is my home, not yours."

"Yes, I know, you're my postmortem tenant. If you think about it, it's really rather funny."

"Funny? What do you mean, 'postmortem tenant'? The owner of this apartment is a woman in her seventies, and very much alive—or at least that's what the Realtor told me."

"She'd love to hear that," she said sarcastically. "She's only sixty-two, although she has aged a lot recently. She's my mother, and for the time being she's my legal guardian. I'm the actual owner."

"You have a legal guardian?"

"Yes. In my present condition, I'm having a tough time signing papers."

"Are you under hospital care?"

"That's putting it mildly."

"Well, they must be very worried about you. Which hospital is it? I'll drive you there."

"Hey, you don't think I'm some nutcase that just escaped from an asylum?"

"No, not . . ."

"Because first you call me a whore and now a nutcase. That's a bit much for a first meeting."

"Listen, I really don't care who you are: whore, nutcase, you could even be some fugitive from *Bewitched*. I'm exhausted and I just want to go to bed and get some sleep."

She ignored him and kept on with her questions. "How do I seem to you?"

"Seem? Disturbed, you seem very disturbed," he said flatly.

"I mean physically. How do I look?"

Arthur hesitated before describing her. He told himself, maybe if he went along with her charade for just a bit, he could get rid of her. And she really was quite striking, he realized as he concentrated on her appearance. "You're rather pretty," he admitted. "You're about average height, rather slender—long legs, I see. Your eyes—" He stopped short. Her eyes were remarkable—an indeterminate color that seemed to be every color at once, almost like the eyes of a newborn. But he wasn't going to get caught up in this folly. "You have a full mouth, pale skin, a pleasing face whose sweetness is in total contrast to your behavior. Your hair is a bit of a mess and could use a good combing out, but it's quite a nice color."

She laughed. "If I asked for directions to Market Street, would you list every building I'd pass on the way?"

"I'm sorry, I don't get the joke."

"Do you always describe women so minutely?"

Arthur felt his anger rising. He was fed up. "How did you get in here? Do you have copies of the keys?"

"I don't need keys. It's so amazing that you can see me.

A miracle. I just can't get it. And your description of me was really very kind, very sweet." She patted the floor beside her. "Please sit down, here beside me. What I have to tell you is not easy to understand, impossible to accept. But if you will listen to my story—if you are willing to trust me—then maybe in the end you'll believe me. And it's very important that you, in particular, should believe me. For without knowing it, you are the only person in the world I can share my secret with."

Arthur sighed, it seemed he had no choice. He must hear what this young woman had to say. So, even though all he wanted was to sleep, he sat down next to her and listened to the most improbable tale he had ever heard in his life.

Her name was Lauren Kline, and she claimed to be a doctor, a medical resident. She told him she had had a car accident six months ago, a serious one, when her steering system failed. "I've been in a coma ever since. No, don't start thinking yet; just let me explain." She had no memory of the accident. She had regained consciousness in the recovery room. Overwhelmed by the strangest sensations, she could hear everything going on around her, but could neither move nor speak. At first she attributed this to anesthesia. "But I was wrong; hours went by, days, and I couldn't wake up physically." She continued to perceive everything but was unable to communicate with the outside world. "That was the most terrifying period of my life: for several days I thought that I was quadriplegic. You have no idea what I went through. A prisoner inside my body for life." Even worse, the outside world—the doctors, her mother, her friends—all seemed to believe that she'd suffered irreversible brain damage.

She had wished with all her might to die, she said, "but it's hard to end it all when you can't even lift your little finger. My mother sat by my bed, day after day, hour after hour, and I begged her with my thoughts to smother me with the pillow." One day a doctor entered the room and she recognized his voice: it was her supervising physician, Alan Fernstein. Mrs. Kline asked him whether her daughter could hear when people spoke to her. Fernstein said he did not know, but studies suggested that comatose patients were indeed sometimes aware of what went on around them. So they should all be careful what they said when they were in her room. "Mom asked him if there was any chance I'd come back one day." Fernstein answered quietly that he still did not know, but that she should hold on to a reasonable measure of hope, because people had been known to emerge from comas even after several months. It was rare, but it happened. "Anything is possible," he said. "We're not gods; we don't know everything. Deep coma is a mystery to medicine."

"I was relieved to hear that," Lauren said. "My body was relatively undamaged. Fernstein was not exactly comforting, but at least he wasn't final, either. Quadriplegia is irreversible," Lauren added. "The weeks dragged on, and on, longer and longer, and soon seemed endless. I lived through them by using my mind and memory to transport myself to other places. In my imagination I'd go everywhere I couldn't go and recount to myself every detail of the places I knew and loved. It was a way to relieve the endless monotony. One night, I was picturing the bustling activity I heard outside my door. I pictured the corridor— the nurses scurrying by, arms full of folders or pushing carts, my colleagues coming and going from one room to another.

"And that's the first time it happened: suddenly, there I

was, in the middle of the corridor I had been visualizing so intently. At first I thought it was my imagination playing tricks. I know the place well; after all, I've worked there for several years. But it all felt so astoundingly real. I could actually see the staff around me: Betty opening the supply-closet door, removing some compresses, and shutting it again; Bill going by scratching his head. It's a nervous tic of his; he does it all the time.

"I could hear the elevator doors, smell the awful meals being served. But no one could see me; people moved to and fro without even trying to avoid me. They walked right through me totally unaware of my presence."

In the next few days she learned to move about the hospital. She would concentrate on imagining the cafeteria and she would be there; or the emergency room, and presto, there she was! After a few weeks of practice she could escape from the hospital. She had shared a meal with a French couple at one of her favorite restaurants, seen half a film in a local theater, and spent several hours in her mother's apartment. "I didn't repeat that visit. It hurt too much to be there, and to see how sad she was, even when she was home. It was bad enough to see her every day at the hospital and be unable to communicate with her. Besides my dog, Kali, had sensed my presence and went running around and around whimpering. I made her crazy. I couldn't handle it. It was just too frustrating, too unbearable. So I came here, to this apartment. After all, it was my home, and I feel best here. I especially love it in the afternoons. I've even gotten used to having you around." She smiled, as though prompting him to say something. He didn't. "I sometimes go back to the hospital to be near my body. If I'm away from it for too long, I become incredibly

33

exhausted. I never sleep, I just rest. I'm always awake, twenty-four hours a day." She looked sad.

"You must understand. I live in total isolation. You can't imagine what it's like not being able to speak to anybody, to be completely transparent, not to exist anymore in everyday life. I'm here, I feel alive, yet I can't affect anything or anyone. So you'll understand my surprise, my exhilaration, when you spoke to me this evening and I realized you could see me. I don't know why, but I only hope it lasts. I could talk to you for hours, I so badly need to talk. I've seen so much, thought so much, been so alone for so long. I've stored up so many things to say." Her rush of words gave way to a moment of silence. She looked at Arthur. "You must think I'm crazy."

Arthur's annoyance had left him; despite himself, he was moved by the young woman's emotion and mesmerized by her bewildering tale.

"No, you don't seem crazy. But this is all very—I don't even know how to put it—disturbing, surprising, extraordinary. I don't know what to say. I'd like to help you, but I don't know how I can."

"Let me stay here. Talk to me, let me live again for a while. I won't bother you."

"You truly believe everything you just told me?"

"You didn't believe a word I said." Her face fell. "Right now, you're telling yourself you have a totally unbalanced girl on your hands. . . . I guess I never stood a chance, did I?"

He asked her to put herself in his place. What would her first reaction be if she discovered a man hiding in her bathroom closet—a somewhat overwrought man, whose explanation was that he was some kind of ghost whose body was in a coma?

Her features relaxed and she smiled a little. She had to

admit that her first reaction would be to scream. She granted him that the circumstances were bizarre.

"But I beg you, Arthur, you must believe me. How could anyone make up such a story?"

"Oh, yes, my business partner could easily dream up a practical joke on this scale."

"Forget your partner, Arthur. He has nothing to do with it. This isn't a joke."

"How do you know my name?"

"Oh, I was here when you looked over the apartment with the Realtor. I was really pleased you liked it so much. I felt very flattered. I remember you signed the lease on the kitchen counter. I was also here when you brought up your boxes and you broke your model airplane." She giggled. "Of course, I'm sorry you broke your toy, but, oh, the cursing and shouting.

"I even watched you hang that hideous painting on the wall, although I admit I used all my willpower to make it fall down, to no avail.

"I was here when you did your obsessive-compulsive number with your drafting table. You must have shifted it twenty times before putting it in the only position it could possibly fit. It was so obvious, I couldn't fathom why it took you so long.

"I've been with you since the first day. The whole time."

"You're here when I take a shower and when I'm in bed?"

"Don't worry. I'm not a voyeur. Although I must say you're quite nicely built. Apart from those love handles— you'll need to keep an eye on those—but aside from that, you're really quite attractive."

Arthur frowned. She was convincing—or rather, had certainly convinced herself—but her story just didn't make sense. If she wanted to believe it, let her. He had no reason to attempt to persuade her she was deluded; he wasn't her therapist, after all. He glanced at the clock. He just wanted to sleep, and despite her wild tale, she seemed harmless enough, so to bring things to a halt he offered to put her up for the night. He would take the couch in the living room, "the one below my hideous attempt at art," and she could take his bedroom. Tomorrow she would go back to where she had come from, to the hospital, or wherever she wanted to go, and that would be the end of it.

But Lauren did not agree. She stood squarely in front of him, her face defiant, determined. Taking a deep breath, she reeled off an astonishing list of all he had said and done in the last few days. She repeated his phone conversation with Carol Ann last Saturday. "She hung up on you right after you lectured her, fairly pompously I must say, about the reasons you don't want to discuss your relationship anymore. *Believe me!*" she begged. Then she reminded him of the two cups he had broken unpacking. *Believe me!* And of how he had overslept and scalded himself in the shower. *Believe me!* She teased him about the time he had spent looking for his keys, throwing a tantrum although nobody was there. She thought he was unobservant because the keys were right there in plain sight, on the little table just inside the front door. *Please believe me.* On Tuesday the phone company came round at 5 P.M. after keeping him waiting for three hours. Then she recalled that he ate a pastrami sandwich, spilled mustard on his coat, and had to change before going out again. "Now do you believe me? I've been living with you for ten days. Don't turn away from me, Arthur, I beg you. I'm a walking miracle. *Believe me!*"

Now he felt exposed, invaded; she had intruded into intimate parts of his life. "You've been spying on me all this time. Why?"

"I haven't been spying on you. Can you see any cameras or microphones in this place?"

"No, I don't, but it would make more sense than your story, wouldn't it?"

"Get your car keys!" she ordered suddenly.

"And where are we going?"

"To the hospital, I'll take you to see me."

"Oh, sure. It's the middle of the night and I'm supposed to schlepp over to a hospital on the other side of town and ask the night nurses to rush me up to the room of a woman I don't know. I'll tell them her ghost is camping out in my apartment, and I really want to get some sleep, but she's dug her heels in, and this is the only way I can get her to leave me in peace."

"Do you know of any other?"

"Any other what?"

"Any other way you're likely to get some sleep."

"Dear God, what did I do to deserve this?"

"You don't believe in God. You said so on the phone to your business partner: 'Paul, I don't believe in God. If we get this contract, it's because we're the best. If we lose it, we'll have to ask ourselves where we went wrong.' Well, consider just for a moment that you might be wrong now. That's all I ask. *Believe me!* I need you. You're my only hope!"

Hearing Lauren mention Paul's name prompted Arthur to pick up the phone and dial his partner's number.

"Paul, did I wake you?"

Paul's voice was groggy and a little annoyed. "No, no, it's the middle of the night and I was waiting for your bed-time call."

"Really? Was I supposed to call you?"

"No, you weren't supposed to call, and yes, you did wake me. What do you want?"

"To hand the phone over to someone and let you know that this time you've gone too far with one of your stupid practical jokes."

Arthur handed the phone to Lauren and asked her to speak to his partner. She could not take the phone, she told him, because she could not hold any solid object. Paul, getting impatient on the other end of the line, asked Arthur whom he was talking to. Arthur smiled in triumph and pressed the button for the speakerphone.

"Can you hear me, Paul?"

"Yes, I can hear you. What is this about? I'd like to get back to sleep."

"I'd like to sleep too, be quiet a second. Speak to him, Lauren, go ahead, speak to him!"

She shrugged. "If you like. Hello, Paul. You most certainly can't hear me. Unlike your partner, who can hear me, but won't listen to me."

"Okay, Arthur, why did you call? If you don't have anything to say, it's really late."

"Answer her."

"Answer who?"

"The person who just spoke to you."

"You're the person who just spoke to me, and now I'm answering."

"You didn't hear anyone else?"

"Tell me, Joan of Arc, have you been working too hard? Are you hallucinating?"

Lauren was staring pityingly at Arthur.

He shook his head. He realized that if this really was one

of Paul's practical jokes, it was too soon for him to call it quits. Arthur told Paul to forget it and apologized for calling so late. Anxiously, Paul asked if everything was all right, and whether he should come over.

Arthur reassured him, "Everything's fine, forget it. Thanks."

"No need to thank me, buddy. If you have a problem, you can wake me anytime with your bullshit, be my guest! We're partners for better or worse. So whenever you're having a bad patch, wake me up and we'll share. Okay, can I go back to sleep or do you have anything else on your mind?"

"Good night, Paul."

They hung up.

"Take me to the hospital, we could have been there by now."

"No, I won't. Because if I do, I'm already halfway to accepting your crazy story. I'm tired and I want to go to bed. So you take my bedroom and I'll take the couch, or else you can leave. That's my last offer."

"You're even more stubborn than I am. Keep your room, I don't need a bed."

"And what will you do?"

"Does it matter?"

"It matters."

"I'll stay right here in the living room."

"Until tomorrow morning. But after that . . ."

"Yes, until tomorrow morning. Thanks for your gracious hospitality!"

"And no spying on me in my bedroom!"

"Since you think I'm faking, just lock your door. If you're concerned because you sleep in the buff, I've already seen you, you know!"

"I thought you weren't a voyeur."

She pointed out that a while ago in the bathroom she would have had to be blind not to see him nude. He cringed and wished her good-night. "You too, Arthur, and sweet dreams."

Arthur slammed the door to his bedroom. "She's mad," he grumbled. He crawled into bed, pulled up the covers, and tried to go to sleep. But of course, he couldn't. He kept going over her appearance, her words, and that bit of doubt kept flaring, especially when he pondered how she'd vaporized from the closet to the living room. Or, he told himself, maybe he was the one going mad. The green numbers on his digital alarm clock indicated one-thirty. He watched the numbers slip by until two-eleven. Then he rose to his feet, pulled on a thick sweater and jeans, and stepped quickly into the living room. Lauren was sitting cross-legged on the window seat. When he came in, she spoke to him without turning around.

"I love this view, don't you? It's what convinced me to buy this apartment. I love looking at the bridge all lit up at night. In the summer I like to open the window and hear the foghorns. I would always dream that I would count the number of waves that break against the ships' bows before they cross the Golden Gate."

"All right, let's go."

"Really? What changed your mind?"

"Since you've already destroyed most of my night, I may as well settle this right now. I'm supposed to work tomorrow. I have an important lunch meeting, and I really need at least four hours' sleep. Can you hurry?"

"Go ahead, I'll join you."

"Where?"

"I said I'll join you. Trust me for just two minutes."

He felt he had already trusted her quite enough. Before he left the house, he asked her again for her last name. She gave it to him, along with the room number where she was supposedly hospitalized: Room 505. It was easy, she said, only fives. But he saw nothing easy in what lay ahead. Arthur locked the door behind him, went down the stairs and into the garage. Lauren was already sitting in the backseat of the car.

"I don't know how you did that, but I'm very impressed. You must have worked with Houdini."

"Who?"

"Houdini, the magician. Come sit up front; I'm not in the mood to play chauffeur on top of everything else."

"Can you try to be a little kind to me? I told you I haven't perfected my aim yet. Even though I focused hard on the inside of the car, I might easily have landed on the hood. So the backseat is pretty good. Trust me, I'm improving."

Lauren came and sat next to him. She looked out the window as Arthur drove through the night. He broke the silence to ask her what he should say once they reached the hospital. She had an idea: "You're my cousin from Argentina. You've just heard the news, and you've got a layover on your flight to England, which leaves at dawn, and you won't be back for six months. That's why it's imperative for them to break the rules and allow you to visit your beloved cousin, despite the late hour." Arthur did not think that he made a convincing Argentinean and predicted that the ruse would not work.

"Don't be so negative," she said. "If worst comes to worst, we'll come back tomorrow." Besides, she explained, they would have a better chance of getting in if they didn't seem to be worried. But Arthur insisted that it was only Lauren's story and wild imagination that was worrying him.

41

The Saab turned into the hospital complex. She told him to make a right, then take the third opening on the left and park just beyond the silver pine. Once they were stopped, she pointed to the night bell, warning him not to ring it too long because it annoyed them.

"Who?" he asked.

"The nurses. They have to come from the far end of a long hall, and they don't know how to teletransport themselves." Arthur just sat there, his head resting on his arms atop the steering wheel.

"Come on, wake up!" Lauren called in his ear.

"I only wish I could," he said ruefully.

Four

Arthur stepped up to the night buzzer and gave it two short rings. A few minutes later, a small woman with round, tortoiseshell glasses opened the door halfway and asked him what he wanted. He stumbled through his lines as best he could. The nurse told him that the hospital had its rules, that rules were meant to be followed: he should simply postpone his flight and return to the hospital the next morning.

He begged. He invoked the importance of the extended family. He invoked the exorbitant cost of international travel. He invoked the exception that was supposed to prove the rule. Nothing worked. He was about to acknowledge defeat when he saw the nurse weaken. She glanced at her watch and said, "I have to do my rounds. Follow me, don't make a sound, don't touch anything, and in fifteen minutes you're out of here." He took her hand and kissed it in token of his gratitude. "Are you all like that in Argentina?" she asked with a slight smile. She opened the door wider to allow him inside. They walked to the elevators and went straight up to the fifth floor.

She opened the door to Room 505. The room was semidark, lit only by a small yellow night-light. From the doorway, Arthur could see a woman lying on the bed, apparently sleeping deeply, but he could not make out her features. The nurse spoke to him in a whisper. "I'll leave the door open, go on in, there's no chance she'll wake up, but be careful what you say, you never know with coma patients. At least that's what the doctors say."

Arthur ventured in cautiously. Lauren was standing by the window and urged him to go up to the bed. "Go on, I'm not going to bite you." As he approached the bed and looked down, he continued asking himself what he was doing there.

The motionless woman was paler than her double, and thinner. Her hands had begun to turn inward in the seizing up that occurs in long-term coma patients, and she looked frail, but the resemblance was striking.

He took a step back. "Are you her twin sister?"

"You're hopeless. I don't have a sister. That's me lying there, no one else but me. No one is playing tricks on you and you aren't dreaming. Arthur, please, you're the only chance I have, you have to help me. Can you imagine what it's like for me to see myself like that, growing paler and more wasted by the day. *Believe me,* Arthur! You're the only person I've been able to communicate with for six months, the only human being who senses I'm here and hears me."

"Why me?"

"I haven't the slightest idea. Maybe because of the apartment? Because you're living in my space? Or maybe there's something special about you. Have you ever had any ESP experiences?"

"Never. I'm a complete rationalist, and this whole thing is really starting to scare me."

"You think I'm not scared?" she asked him plaintively. Of fear, she'd had more than her fair share. She had watched her own body gradually withering away, lying there with an IV drip to irrigate her, a feeding tube to nourish her, and a catheter to carry away her waste. She could move about all over the city, invisible, but she couldn't so much as make her own body's eyelids flutter. She had no way to explain to him how this was possible; she could no more answer his questions than she could answer those she had asked herself every day since the accident. "You can't even begin to imagine what goes through my mind." With a forlorn look, she confided in him her doubts and worries. "I ask myself, how long can this mystery possibly last? Why has this happened to me, of all people? I'm a scientist, not a whacked-out psychic who's been trying to astral-project since the sixties. How did I get trapped here, separate from my body? How can I get back? Will I ever be able to lead a normal life again, even for just a few days, walking on my own two legs, talking to the people I love and having them hear me, touching them with my own hands and having them feel my touch? It's torture, believe me.

"I don't know how many days I have left before my heart gives out. At first, people came to visit often; friends and colleagues from the hospital would stop by several times a day—and they'd all talk to me, they all tried to talk me back from the coma. But that was only for the first few weeks. Now my friends have stopped coming, my colleagues still look in, but they don't talk to me as if they believe I could possibly wake up anymore. Only my mother valiantly holds on, but I can tell she's weakening. I've heard the doctors and nurses speculating on how long the hospital will let me keep this room—in an ordinary situation, they would have transferred me to an extended-care facility after a few weeks.

"You must understand, Arthur, I've been here watching myself die. I'm terrified and I'm all alone. You're my first ray of hope. Do you know how wonderful it is to have someone hear me? To be able to talk and have you respond? To be able to feel it when you touch me? You're my only human contact. I may be a ghost, Arthur, but I'm a human ghost."

He lowered his gaze, avoiding her desperate eyes. "To die you have to leave first, and you're still here," he murmured.

They remained silent for a long time, then he took her hand. "Come, let's go home. I'm tired and so are you. Come back with me."

He put his arm across her shoulders and pulled her toward him comfortingly. Turning around, he found himself face-to-face with the nurse, who was looking at him with dismay.

"Are you okay?"

"Yes, why?"

"Your arm in the air like that, your fingers curled, it looks like you have some sort of cramp."

Arthur hurriedly removed his hand from Lauren's shoulder and let his arm fall by his side. "You can't see her, can you?"

"Can't see who?"

"No one."

"Would you like to rest before you leave? All of a sudden you seem a little overwrought." The nurse tried to soothe him. "It's always such a shock to see a loved one in a coma. It's to be expected that you're discombobulated. Why don't you sit down and relax a minute."

Arthur spoke slowly, as if searching for lost words. "No, really, I'm fine. I'll just go now." The nurse was concerned that he might not be able to find his way back. Pulling himself together, Arthur reassured her that he could: the exit was just at the end of the hall.

"I'll say good-bye here then."

Arthur said good-bye and started down the corridor.

The nurse saw him lift his arm back to the horizontal and heard him mumble, "I believe you, Lauren, I believe you."

The nurse frowned and went into the next room. "Some people get so shaken up, there's just nothing you can say."

Arthur and Lauren headed out of the hospital together in silence. A north wind had blown in from the ocean bringing with it drizzling rain. It was suddenly quite cold. Arthur pulled his coat collar up and opened the car door for Lauren. "We're going to have to lighten up a little on the walking-through-walls act, do you mind?"

She climbed into the car in the conventional way and smiled at him.

Neither uttered a word on the way back. Arthur concentrated on the road, trying to keep at bay the thousands of questions that were flooding his mind, while Lauren watched the clouds scudding over the night sky. Only when they were nearly home did she speak, without turning her face from the window.

"I used to love the night for its silence, all those shapes without shadows, the looks of strangers you never catch during the daytime. It's as if two separate worlds share the same city without knowing each other, without imagining the existence of the other. So many people come out at night and disappear with the dawn.

No one knows where they go. The hospital personnel, the late-night workers—we're the only ones who know them."

"Lauren, you've got to admit this all seems impossible."

"Yes, but please let's not spend the rest of the night discussing it."

"You mean, what's left of my night!"

Arthur parked the car on the street to avoid waking his neighbors with the noise of the garage door. Slowly, he went upstairs and into his apartment. Lauren was already sitting cross-legged in the middle of the living room.

"Did you aim for the couch?" he asked, amused.

"No, I aimed for the carpet and landed right on target."

"You're bluffing, I bet you aimed for the couch."

"And I'm telling you I aimed for the rug!"

"Liar."

"I would love to be able to make you some tea, but . . . you should go on to bed."

Arthur sighed and turned toward the bedroom, again offering Lauren the bed. "Really, I don't mind sleeping on the couch," he assured her. She thanked him for his gallantry, but the couch was fine. He went to bed too tired to think about all of the evening's implications; there would be time for that tomorrow.

Before he closed the door he wished her good-night, and she asked him one last favor: "Would you mind giving me a hug?" Arthur cocked his head coyly. "It's been six months since anyone held me." He walked over, took her by the shoulders, and pulled her into the circle of his arms. She rested her head against his chest. They stood like that for a few minutes. Arthur felt awkward, at a loss. She felt fragile, and a bit cold, but she felt real. Clumsily, he dropped his hands to her slender waist. She brushed his shoulder with her cheek.

"Thank you, Arthur, thank you for everything. Go to sleep now; you must be exhausted. I'll wake you at eight."

He went to his bedroom, peeled off sweater and shirt, tossed his pants on a chair, and crawled under the covers. Moments later he was asleep.

Lauren remained in the living room until she assumed he was asleep, then she shut her eyes, concentrated, and made a wobbly landing on the arm of the big chair facing the bed. For a long time, she watched him. Arthur's face looked peaceful; she could even see the beginnings of a smile at the corners of his mouth. How good it was to connect with another human being at last. She gazed at him until slumber overwhelmed her too.

Five

W HEN LAUREN AWOKE, IT WAS TEN O'CLOCK; ARTHUR was still fast asleep. "Oh my God!" she said loudly, and sat down beside the bed, shaking him vigorously. "Wake up!"

He turned over, protesting, "Take it easy, Carol Ann."

"Charming. Absolutely charming. Wake up, this isn't Carol Ann, and it's already past ten."

At first Arthur's eyelids parted slowly, then they snapped wide open and he jolted upright.

"You're disappointed? You'd prefer Carol Ann?"

"It's you. So, it wasn't a dream?"

"You could have spared me that line. It's awfully predictable. Come on. You'd better hurry, you're late for work."

"You were supposed to wake me."

"I'm sorry, I fell asleep, which hasn't happened to me since the accident. What a relief! I was hoping we could celebrate, but obviously you're not in the mood."

"Don't use that sarcastic tone with me. You kept me up

all night, and now I'm going to be late. If you'd be so kind . . ."

"You're so gracious in the morning, I think I like you better asleep."

"You're not going to make a scene, are you?"

"Don't even think about it. Go on, get dressed."

"I'd love to. Now, would you mind leaving the room so I can have a little privacy, please."

"So all of a sudden you've gotten prudish?"

He pleaded with her to spare him the household drama and was foolhardy enough to finish his sentence with "or else."

"Sometimes *or else* are two words too many," she shot back. Coldly wishing him a good day, she vanished.

Arthur looked all around, hesitated for a moment, then called out, "Lauren? I know you're here somewhere. Come on out, this is ridiculous." As he stood there, in his boxers, he caught the eye of his neighbor across the street, who was watching the scene from his window. Arthur grabbed a blanket, wrapped it around his waist, and headed for the bathroom, muttering, "I've never been this late before. I'm half-naked in the middle of my room, talking to a ghost. Okay, buddy, you tell me. What the hell is going on?"

In the bathroom he opened the closet door and asked softly, "Lauren, are you there?" Again there was no reply, and he was disappointed. He showered at top speed. When he finished, he returned to the bedroom, checked for Lauren in the other closet, and not finding her, put on his suit. He had to make three attempts at knotting his tie. Once dressed, he went to the kitchen and searched the counter for his keys, but finally found them in his pocket. He hurried from the apartment, stopped in his tracks, turned about, and opened the door again. "Lauren, still not there?" After a few seconds' silence, he double-locked the door. Taking the outside stairs straight to the garage, he looked for his car. Remembering that he had parked it in the street, he ran back down the hallway and finally reached the sidewalk. Raising his eyes, he saw his neighbor again, staring at him with a puzzled look. He gave him an embarrassed smile, fumbled with the key as he unlocked the car door, sat behind the wheel, and roared away.

When Arthur reached the office, Paul was standing in the reception area, clad, as always, in black from head to toe. And as always, his hair, shaggy around his ears and beginning to bald on top, looked electrified. He nodded disparagingly when he saw Arthur and, with a wry expression on his face, said, "Maybe you should take a few days off."

"Eat it. Don't piss me off this morning, Paul."

"Charming—absolutely charming."

"What is it with everyone this morning. Don't you get at me too."

"You've seen Carol Ann again?"

"No, I haven't seen Carol Ann. It's over with her, and you know it."

"There are only two explanations for the state you're in: Carol Ann or a new one."

"No, there isn't a new one. Now move, I'm late enough already."

"No kiddin'. After all, it's only a quarter of eleven. What's her name?"

"Whose?"

"Have you seen your face this morning?"

"What's the matter with it?"

"Come on. How was it? Tell me."

"I have nothing to tell."

"And your late-night call, with all that bullshit, who was she?"

Arthur stared at his partner. "Look, I ate some bad seafood last night, and then I had a nightmare, I got very little sleep. Please, I'm really not in the mood. Let me get by, I'm late."

Paul moved aside. As Arthur passed him, Paul patted his shoulder. "I'm your friend, aren't I?" Arthur turned, and Paul added, "You'd tell me if you were in trouble?"

"I slept badly last night, that's all. Don't make a thing out of it."

"Fine, fine. Lunch is at one, we're meeting at the top of the Hyatt Embarcadero. We can go together if you like. I'm coming back to the office afterward."

"No, I'll take my car. I have another meeting this afternoon."

"Whatever."

Arthur entered his office, put his briefcase on the desk, sat down, called his secretary, asked her for a coffee, swiveled his chair around to face the window, leaned backward, and tried to think.

A few moments later Maureen tapped on the door. She was dressed matronly in a tailored blue suit and sensible shoes. She carried a thick folder in one hand, and a cup of coffee with a doughnut balanced on the edge of the saucer in the other. She set the cup and saucer on a corner of the table and sat in the chair beside his desk.

"I put milk in it. I imagine it's your first of the day."

"Thanks." He paused for a second. "Uh, Maureen, how do I look?"

"You've got a 'Haven't had my first coffee yet' look."

"I haven't had my first coffee yet!"

"Okay, relax. Take your time over breakfast. You have a bunch of messages, but there's nothing urgent, just these letters to be signed." She paused and eyed him suspiciously. "Are you okay?"

"Yes, a bit tired, that's all."

At that precise moment, Lauren materialized in the room. Narrowly missing the corner of the desk, she disappeared from Arthur's line of sight, falling on the rug beyond his desk. He leapt to his feet.

"Did you hurt yourself?"

"No, no, I'm okay," said Lauren.

"Why would I have hurt myself?" asked Maureen.

"No, not you," Arthur said.

Maureen glanced around the room. "There aren't that many of us here."

"I was thinking out loud."

"You were thinking out loud that I'd hurt myself?"

"No, I was thinking about someone else, and I said my thoughts out loud. Doesn't that ever happen to you?"

Lauren, now sitting with legs crossed on the edge of the table, decided to goad Arthur a little. "You didn't have to compare me to a nightmare when you were talking to Paul just now."

"I never called you a nightmare."

"I'm very glad to hear it," said Maureen. "How many nightmares bring you a cup of coffee in the morning?"

"Maureen, I'm not talking to you!"

"Then either there's a ghost in the room or else I've gone blind and I'm missing something. Which is it?"

"I'm sorry. It's ridiculous. I'm ridiculous. I'm exhausted and I'm thinking out loud. My mind's a million miles away."

"You've been working too hard, Arthur. You finished

the Murphy restoration and went right into the Aliotto design and moved all in two months. Have you ever heard of burnout? You have to act at the first signs or it can take months to recover."

"Maureen, I'm not suffering from burnout. I just had a bad night, that's all."

Lauren broke in, "There you are: bad night, nightmare!"

"Stop it, please. I have to concentrate. Just be quiet for a few minutes."

"But I didn't say anything!" Maureen exclaimed.

"Maureen, please go back to your desk. I have to pull myself together. I'll do some breathing exercises, some relaxation exercises, and I'll be fine."

"Relaxation exercises? You're scaring me, Arthur, you really are."

"There's no reason to be scared. I'm fine, I assure you. Now, just leave me alone—and hold all my calls. I just need a bit of peace and quiet and solitude."

Maureen reluctantly left the room, closing the door behind her.

Alone in his office, Arthur stared at Lauren. "You've got to cut the *Bewitched* act, Lauren. You're putting me in an impossible position."

"I wanted to apologize for this morning. I shouldn't have gone off in a huff like that. I know how hard it is for you to deal with all this."

"I'm sorry, I was the one in a lousy mood. It's just been a lot to take in in a very short time."

"Let's not spend the morning trading apologies. I wanted to talk to you."

Just then, Paul opened the door and came into the office. "Could I have a word with you?"

"You are already, aren't you?"

"I've just spoken with Maureen; Arthur, what's wrong, what's going on with you?"

"Nothing. Just because I'm tired and arrived late for once doesn't mean I'm having a nervous breakdown."

"I didn't say you were."

"No, but that's what Maureen suggested. Apparently I look like a zombie this morning."

"Putting it mildly. Jesus, you really look like you had a rough night."

"It was a bit wild," Arthur admitted, trying to decide how much to tell Paul.

"I knew it! I knew there must be a woman involved in all this."

Arthur nodded, raising his brows.

"Aha! You see, you can't keep anything from me. I was sure! Anyone I know?"

"No, no way."

"Tell me about her. Who is she? When do I get to meet her?"

"It'll be tricky, Paul. I know this sounds sort of strange, but she's kind of a ghost. My apartment is haunted. I found out by accident last night. She was living in my bathroom closet. I spent the night with her, but it was all very inno-cent. She's pretty—as ghosts go—not—" Arthur hunched his shoulders, imitating a monster. "Really, she's very pretty for someone who's come back from the dead, and in fact she hasn't really returned from the dead. She's in a dif-ferent category because she hasn't completely died. Are things clearer now?"

Paul looked sympathetically at his partner. "Right. Look, Arthur, I think you need to see a doctor right away."

"Stop it, Paul, I assure you I'm absolutely fine." Arthur turned to Lauren. "You see, this isn't going to be easy."

"What's not going to be easy?" asked Paul.

"I wasn't talking to you."

"You were talking to the ghost? Is it here in the room?"

Arthur reminded him that "it" was a she, adding that she was sitting next to Arthur on the edge of the table. Paul looked doubtfully at him and slowly ran the palm of his hand across his partner's desk.

"Listen, I know I sometimes go a bit far with my practical jokes, but this time, Arthur, you're going completely overboard. You're scaring me. You can't see yourself, but you look as if you're at the end of your rope this morning."

"I'm tired, I barely slept. I'm sure I look awful, but inside I'm in great shape. I promise you, everything's just fine."

"You're in great shape inside? Well, the front of you seems in pretty bad shape; what about the sides?"

"Paul, let me get on with my work. You're my friend, not my therapist. I mean, I don't even have a therapist."

Paul asked him not to come to their one-o'clock signature meeting on the Swope deal. If he did, Paul warned Arthur, he might lose them the contract. "I don't believe you realize the state you're in. You're sort of frightening."

Irritated, Arthur rose, picked up his briefcase, and walked to the door.

"Okay, I'm scary. I look crazy. Fine, I'll go home. Get out of my way, Paul. Come on, Lauren, we're out of here!"

"Brilliant, Arthur. You're a genius. That ghost number is a real whopper."

"It's not a number, Paul. You're too—what's the word?—conventional to understand what I'm experiencing. But you'll notice that I don't hold it against you. I've come a long way myself since last night."

"Listen to yourself. It's mind-blowing!"

"Yes, so you've already said. Listen, don't worry about a thing. It's good that you're offering to handle the meeting by yourself. I really didn't get much sleep, so I'm going to get some rest, thank you very much. I'll be back tomorrow, and everything will be much better."

Paul suggested that Arthur take a few days off, at least until the end of the week. Moving was always stressful. Paul would be happy to help Arthur over the weekend, if he needed anything at all. Arthur thanked Paul with a tinge of sarcasm, then left the room and ran down the stairs. Stepping out onto the sidewalk, he looked around for Lauren.

"Are you there?"

Lauren appeared, sitting on the hood of his car. "I'm creating a whole load of problems for you. I'm really sorry."

"No, don't be. The fact is, I haven't done this for ages."

"Done what?"

"Skipped work. Just think, an entire day playing hooky!"

Standing at the office window, brow creased, Paul watched his partner talk to himself in the street, open the passenger door for no reason and then close it again, walk around the car, and climb in behind the wheel. Paul didn't know what to do; Arthur was not only Paul's partner, he was his best friend. They had met at school and had hit it off immediately. They had much in common—they were both only children who had lost their fathers when they were very young, had been raised by their mothers and then sent off to boarding schools. As a result, they both valued friendship highly, were loyal to a fault, loved pranks, and had a zest for life. After graduating, they both went to work at MOMA, and two years later they had formed a partnership, specializing in Victorian restorations. Buoyed by San Francisco's housing boom, their firm acquired a solid reputation for fairness, timeliness, and taste. Paul looked after the construction and the business end of things; Arthur designed—furniture and interiors. Each man was comfortable and confident in his role, and in five years of partnership there had never been even a shadow of true conflict in their relationship. Paul had never seen Arthur so unhinged. Something was wrong, he was convinced of it. His best friend was either having a breakdown or was well on the way to a stress-induced stroke.

Sitting in the driver's seat, Arthur put his hands on the wheel and sighed. He looked at Lauren and smiled, saying nothing.

A bit embarrassed, she returned his smile. "It's frustrating having someone think you're crazy, isn't it? At least he didn't call you a whore!"

"Why didn't he get it?" Arthur said facetiously. "Wasn't my explanation clear?"

"Clear as crystal. What now?"

"Breakfast, and then you can tell me everything, in detail."

From his office window, Paul continued to watch his friend, parked below on the other side of the street. When he saw him talking to himself in the car, chatting with an invisible and imaginary character, he decided to call him on his cell phone. When Arthur answered, Paul asked him not to start the car, he would be right down, he had to talk to him.

"What about?" asked Arthur.

"That's why I'm coming down!"

Paul ran down the stairs, crossed the street, opened the Saab's driver's door, and almost sat on his best friend's lap.

"Move over!"

"Get in on the other side, for God's sake!"

"Do you mind if I do the driving?"

"I don't get it. Are we talking or going for a ride?"

"Both. Come on, change seats!"

Pushing Arthur over, Paul settled behind the wheel, turned the key, and the car moved away from the curb. At the first intersection he braked hard.

"First things first: Is your ghost with us in the car right now?"

"Yes, she moved into the backseat, after your cavalier entrance."

Paul opened his door, got out, tilted his seat forward, and said to Arthur, "Do me a favor. Ask Casper to get out of the car and leave us alone for a while. I have to have a private talk with you. You can catch up with each other at your place."

Lauren reappeared outside the passenger window. "Pick me up at North Point. I'll be taking a walk there. You know, if it's too complicated, you don't need to tell him the truth."

"He's my friend and my partner, I can't lie to him."

"Go ahead, discuss me with your glove compartment," said Paul. "Why, just last night I opened the refrigerator, saw a light inside, and so I went in and talked about you with the butter and a head of lettuce for a good half hour."

"I'm not discussing you with the glove compartment. I'm talking to her."

"Well, then, please ask Lady Casper to go iron her sheet so that you and I can talk in peace."

Lauren vanished.

"Did it leave?" Paul asked a little anxiously.

"It's *she,* not it! Yes, she's gone. You're so rude. Now, what's up with you?"

"What's up with *me?*" repeated Paul, making a face. He turned the engine back on and headed down Sutter Street. "I just wanted to be alone so I could talk about some personal matters with you."

"Like what?"

"The delayed reactions that sometimes set in after a breakup."

Paul launched into a long tirade. Carol Ann wasn't right for Arthur. In his view, she had hurt Arthur badly, and *she wasn't worth it.* When all was said and done, the woman was *emotionally handicapped* and *didn't know how to be happy.* Was she honestly worth what Arthur had gone through since their separation? He hadn't been *wasted this way* since Karin. Now Karin, she was a real loss, whereas frankly Carol Ann . . .

Arthur pointed out that at the time of the famous Karin they were only nineteen, and for the record, he added, he had never hit on her. For almost fifteen years now Paul had been bringing her up on the slimmest of pretexts, simply because Arthur had seen her first. Paul denied ever mentioning her. "At least two or three times a year!" Arthur retorted. "Presto! And out she pops, a flash from the past. I can't even remember her face!"

Paul, suddenly annoyed, began to wave his arms. "Then why won't you tell me the truth about her? Admit it for God's sake, you went out with her! It's been fifteen years, as you say. The statute of limitations has expired."

"You're getting on my nerves, Paul! You didn't come racing downstairs and we're not driving across town because all of a sudden you want to discuss Karin Pearson!"

"You can't remember her face but you haven't forgotten her last name!"

"Is this the important personal matter you wanted to talk about?"

"No, I'm talking about Carol Ann."

"Why? I haven't seen her and we haven't talked on the phone since the time I told you about a week ago. If that's what's worrying you, it doesn't warrant us driving to Los Angeles—because in case you haven't noticed, we're already in South Market. So what do you want? And why have we driven halfway across town?"

Paul turned left and drove the Saab into the parking area of a big four-story building with a white-tiled facade.

"Paul, I know it'll seem crazy to you, but I really have met a ghost."

"Arthur, I know it'll seem crazy to you, but I really am taking you for a medical checkup."

Arthur, who had been looking at his friend, swiftly turned his head to stare at the name on the front of the building. "You're taking me to this clinic? Seriously? You don't believe me?"

"Of course I believe you! And I'll believe you even more when you've seen a doctor and had some tests."

"You want me to have medical tests?"

"Listen to me, you big lug! If I arrive at the office one day looking like someone stuck on an escalator for a month, and then I leave in a rage even though I never lose my temper, and then you see me from your window opening my car door for a nonexistent passenger, and, not content with that, continuing to talk and wave my hands around inside my car as if I'm talking to someone, but there's no one, really no one, and all I can offer you by way of explanation is that I've just met a ghost, I hope you'll be as concerned for me as I am for you right now."

Arthur managed a smile. "When I met her in my closet, I thought it was one of your jokes."

"Come on, follow me, we're going to put my mind at rest now."

Arthur let himself be dragged by the arm to the clinic reception area. The receptionist watched them as Paul sat Arthur on a chair and told him not to move. Paul was treating Arthur the way you treat an unruly child you don't want to let out of your sight.

Then Paul walked to the desk and said urgently to the young woman, "This is an emergency!"

"What kind of emergency?" she asked, her voice distinctly casual in contrast to Paul's impatient tone.

"The kind sitting in the chair, the one over there."

"No, I'm asking the nature of the emergency."

"Cranial shock."

"How did it happen?"

"Love is blind, and repeated blows on the head with a long white cane seem to have rattled his brain."

She found the answer funny, without being really certain she'd understood it.

"We need to see Dr. Bresnick," Paul insisted.

"I'm sorry but Dr. Bresnick is in clinic at the hospital today. I'll be happy to make you an appointment for tomorrow."

Arthur called Paul aside. "Listen, Paul, this is ridiculous. I'm fine. I assure you there's nothing physically wrong with me. I'm just stressed-out. You're right, I need to take some time off, walk along the beach, smell the flowers. I'll take the week off. There's nothing pressing, now that I've finished the Aliotto design. Trust me, buddy, really, I'm okay. I just need some rest."

Paul looked at Arthur suspiciously. "You know I love you, man. I'm worried about you. Promise you'll call me tomorrow and we can get out of here."

"I promise. Now I'll take you back to the office."

Reluctantly Paul agreed. "But we need to talk about this later. I'd better go straight to the meeting; I'll take a cab. I'll call you tonight."

Paul left him alone in the Saab. Arthur drove quickly toward North Point. He had to admit, deep inside, he was beginning to like this story, its heroine, and the situations it was bound to provoke.

Six

THE SEA-VIEW RESTAURANT SAT PERCHED ON A CLIFF overlooking the Pacific and Seal Rocks. Its dining area was almost full, and two TV screens over the bar allowed patrons to watch two different football games at once. The bets were rolling. Lauren and Arthur sat behind a glass bay window.

The waitress, a young, obviously wanna-be actress, greeted him and asked if he'd like something to drink. He was about to order a Virgin Mary when he was startled by a tickling sensation. Suddenly, Lauren was stroking his leg with her bare foot, eyes full of mischief, a triumphant smile on her face. Responding in kind, he grabbed her ankle and ran his hand up the length of her leg.

"I can feel you too!" he exclaimed.

"I wanted to be sure."

"You are now."

The waitress looked dubiously at him. "What can you feel?"

"Nothing. I don't feel anything."

"You just said, 'I can feel you too.' "

He turned to Lauren, now flashing a brilliant smile. "I could get myself locked up for this."

"Maybe that's not such a bad idea," said the waitress, turning on her heel.

"Hey, can you take my order?" he yelled after her.

"I'll send over Bob. We'll see if you can feel him too."

Bob, if anything more feminine than his colleague, appeared a few minutes later. Arthur ordered scrambled eggs with salmon, paused a second, and opted for a *Bloody* Mary. This time he waited for the waiter to leave before he spoke to Lauren. "Now, tell me everything again, from the beginning."

Bob halted in the middle of the room, looking askance as his customer started talking to the empty seat across from him. Lauren cut Arthur off in midsentence to ask if he had his cell phone with him. Not grasping her intent, he nodded.

"Take it out and pretend to be speaking into it; otherwise they really will lock you up."

Arthur looked around and realized that people at several tables had stopped eating and were staring at him, disconcerted by this person chatting alone. He grabbed his phone, punched in a number, and said, "Hello!" very loud. People went on staring at him for a few seconds. Once everything seemed more or less normal, they resumed their meals. He asked his question again into the mouthpiece.

"When this began," she told him, "when I realized I could move around in space, transparency was rather fun. It gave me a feeling of absolute freedom. No more worries about how to dress or how to wear my hair, or how my face or figure appeared: nobody looked at me anymore. No more obligations, no more routine, and no more waiting in line. And your favorite part," she said with a playful smile, "I didn't have to respect anyone's privacy: I could eavesdrop on conversations, see the invisible, hear the inaudible, go where I had no right to be."

Bob arrived with the meal, set it before Arthur, all the while looking at him as if he were about to spring up and do something loony. Arthur ate with one hand, phone pressed to his ear with his other as he listened.

"I can go and sit on the corner of the Oval Office desk and listen to all the state secrets, cuddle on Richard Gere's lap, or take a shower with Tom Cruise."

Everything, or almost everything, was possible. She could visit museums and boutiques when they were closed, enter a movie theater without paying, sleep in palaces, go for a spin in a fighter plane, observe the most advanced surgery, secretly visit research labs, swing on the cables of the Golden Gate's bridge. Arthur, ear glued to his cell phone, was curious to know whether she had tried at least one of those experiences.

"No, except for movies. I suffer from vertigo, I hate planes. Washington, D.C.'s too far; I don't yet know how to transport myself long distances. As for sleeping in palaces, yesterday was the first time I've slept since this happened. And finally, what's the point of shopping when you can't touch anything?"

"What about Richard Gere and Tom Cruise?"

"Same thing as for the shopping . . ." She smiled.

She told him with great earnestness that it was no fun at all being a ghost. In fact, she was miserable. Everything was within her reach but impossible to grasp. She missed her friends, her work, the routine of her life. When her distraught friends visited her in the hospital, she could do nothing to reassure them. And her mother was a constant worry. She was in agony, sitting for hours every day by her silent, motionless daughter's side, and Lauren could not comfort her. "I no longer exist. I can see her and hear her, but I can't touch her, and that hurts more than it helps. Maybe that's what purgatory is, everlasting loneliness. I really am in limbo, neither dead nor truly alive."

"Did you see any white light or anything, like they say in the near-death books?"

"No, none of that. I just woke up suddenly in the hospital."

"Do you believe in God?"

"No, I've never been religious. But in my current situation you start to question all your old beliefs. I never believed in ghosts either."

"Neither do I," he said.

"You don't believe in ghosts?"

"You're not really a ghost."

"I'm not?"

"You're not dead, Lauren. Your heart is beating in one place, and your spirit is alive somewhere else. They've temporarily separated, amazing as it seems. We have to find out why, then try to bring them back together."

"You'll agree that it's a divorce with awfully heavy consequences."

This was all way beyond his sphere of comprehension, but he did not intend to leave it at that. His phone still pressed to his ear, he told her he wanted to learn more.

They had to find a way to get her back into her body; otherwise she would never come out of her coma. The two things had to be linked, he added.

"I believe you've made a breakthrough in your research, Doctor!"

He ignored her sarcasm and suggested that they go home and search the Web. He wanted to read every article pertaining to coma: scientific studies, medical reports, bibliographies, stories, eyewitness accounts. He was particularly interested in people who had returned after being in a long-term coma. Hell, he was even ready to read all those life-beyond-death books, talk to all those types he had only yesterday considered completely wacko. "We have to track them down and question them. What they tell us could be very important."

"Why are you doing this?" She was looking at him skeptically.

"Because you sure can't."

"Answer my question. Do you realize the implications of what you're proposing, how long it could take you? You have your career, your own obligations."

"First you want my help, then you don't. You're a woman of contradictions."

"No, I simply see things more clearly now. Didn't you notice that people were looking at you like you were crazy because you were alone at this table talking to yourself? Do you realize that next time you come to this restaurant they'll tell you they're full?"

"This city has more than a thousand restaurants. There are tons of them left."

"Arthur, you're very kind, but I'm afraid you're being unrealistic."

"I don't mean to hurt your feelings, but you're hardly in a position to accuse someone else of being unreal."

"Don't play with my words . . . or with me. You'll never be able to figure this out. The truth is, you simply won't have time."

"I hate doing this in a restaurant, but you give me no choice. Excuse me a second."

Arthur pretended to hang up, looked into her eyes, picked up the phone again, and called his partner's number. He thanked Paul for his concern, for trying to help, for the time he had spent with him that morning. He had given it a lot of thought and concluded that Paul was right. He was indeed on the brink of a nervous breakdown brought on by overwork, and it was best for the firm and for him if he took more than a week off. He was thinking more like a month. As Maureen had pointed out, he had a lull right now. Paul could finalize the Aliotto plan, which was the only one Arthur had pending. And he'd check in every couple of days. He gave Paul some specific information about other bids they had in and told him Maureen was at his disposal. He was too tired to go away anywhere. He would be at home and could be reached on the phone.

"There," he said as he clicked off the phone. "I'm now free of all professional obligations, and I suggest we begin our research at once."

"Why have you changed so much since last night? Why are you suddenly willing to risk everything to help me? I don't understand."

"Now, I'm going to tell you a story, and then you'll understand. One evening my mother had a dinner party. I couldn't have been more than ten. One of the guests was a famous eye surgeon, a Dr. Coburn Miller; everyone called him Coco. He seemed strangely quiet and preoccupied, which was out of character. My mother asked him what was wrong."

Two weeks before, Dr. Miller had operated on a little girl blind since birth. She did not know what she looked like, had no concept of the sky, could not imagine colors, had never seen even her own mother's face. The outside world was unknown to her, no external image had ever entered her brain. She could only guess what things looked like by the shapes and contours she felt with her hands.

Coco gambled everything on an intricate and risky operation, an "impossible" operation. Two weeks later, which happened to be the morning of the dinner party, it was time to remove the bandages. He was alone with the little girl in her hospital room.

"You'll start to see things before I'm through taking off these dressings. Are you ready?"

"What am I going to see?" she asked.

"I've already told you, you'll see light."

"But what's light?"

"It's life. . . . I can't describe it, but wait a moment."

And a few seconds later, just as he had promised, the light of day entered her eyes. For the first time the millions of cells in her retinas were stimulated by light, triggering a wonderfully complex chemical reaction that would codify the images imprinted upon them and instantaneously transmit them to the two optic nerves, just roused from dormancy and able to pass this enormous volume of information to the brain. The most ancient of all image processors, the most complex and the smallest in the world, had suddenly been linked to an optical system and was now at work. The little girl took Coco's hand and said,

"Wait, I'm scared." He stopped removing the dressings, took her in his arms, and told her all over again what would happen when he was through. Hundreds of new items of information to absorb, understand, and compare with everything her imagination had constructed. Then Coco resumed his removal of the bandages.

When she opened her eyes, she looked first at her hands; she moved them up and down and sideways as though she were moving puppets. She tipped her head to one side, smiled, laughed, wept too, and could not tear her eyes away from her ten fingers. Perhaps she concentrated on her hands because everything around her was appearing all at the same time. It was too much too soon, and she was terrified. Then she directed her gaze at her rag doll, which had kept her company night and day in total darkness.

The door opened at the far end of the big room, and her mother came in without saying a word. The little girl raised her head and looked. She had never seen her mother before! And yet, the child's face changed and she opened her arms wide and without a moment's hesitation called this "stranger" Mommy.

"When Coco finished telling his story," continued Arthur, "I realized that for the rest of his life he would possess a tremendous strength: he had done something truly important. I remember promising myself right there, if such an opportunity ever came to me, I would take it. So let's just say that you're my opportunity, the one I've been waiting for, for more than twenty years. And what I'm doing for you is in memory of Coco Miller."

Lauren was silent. She simply smiled at Arthur and reached across the table and took both his hands in hers.

Bob arrived with the check, watching Arthur warily.

Arthur popped his eyes wide open, made a frightening face, stuck his tongue out, and sprang to his feet. Bob took a step back.

"I expected better of you, Bob, I'm very disappointed. Come, Lauren, this place is unworthy of us."

In the car on the way back to the apartment, Arthur outlined the methods he intended to use in his investigation. They exchanged ideas and agreed on a course of action.

Seven

Back at home, Arthur sat down at his worktable. He turned on his computer and logged on to the Internet. The information superhighway gave him instant access to hundreds of databases on the subject he wanted to explore. He clicked on a search engine, then simply typed the word *coma* in the appropriate box. His search yielded several sites containing articles, first-person stories, and analyses. There was even a news group with person-to-person exchanges on the subject. Lauren settled onto the corner of the desk so she could read everything along with him.

Their first step was to link up to Memorial Hospital's Web page, where they selected the heading "Neuropathology and Cerebral Traumatology." This led them to a recent article on cranial trauma by a Dr. Silverstone. In it, he explained the classification of the different degrees of consciousness, according to the Glasgow Scale. A series of three digits indicated the degree to which patients reacted to visual, auditory, and sensory stimuli. The digits corresponding to Lauren's case were 1.1.2., which added up to a class four coma, otherwise known as an "irreversible" coma. Arthur then accessed another site, containing a statistical analysis of patient outcomes in each class of coma. No one had ever returned from a voyage in "fourth class."

A number of diagrams, cross-sections of nerves, drawings, case histories, treatment protocols, and bibliographical sources were downloaded into Arthur's computer, then printed. All told, nearly seven hundred pages of information were sorted and classified according to topic.

Arthur ordered a pizza and two beers and announced that there was nothing left to do but read. Again, Lauren asked him why he was doing all this. He answered, "Out of gratitude to someone who has given me a great deal in very little time, the most important thing of all being a renewed sense of excitement and wonder." Then he returned to his reading, making margin notes beside passages he didn't understand, which was almost all of them. As they went along, Lauren explained the terminology and various medical facts and theories to him.

Arthur pinned a large sheet of paper to his architect's table and began to synthesize all the information he had collected. Grouping similar data into one category, he then circled it and linked it to related categories. Gradually a huge diagram appeared on the page, spilling onto a second sheet of paper where the data and information were transformed into conclusions.

They spent two days and two nights trying to understand and come up with a key to the enigma confronting them.

Two days and two nights to conclude that, in spite of the advances of modern medicine, the coma remained a mystery, a dark zone in which the body lived divorced from the mind that animated it and gave it a soul. It would take more years than they had, and many more researchers, to unlock the mystery. Exhausted, eyes reddened, Arthur fell asleep on the floor.

Lauren, sitting at the architect's table, pored over the diagrams, her fingertips following the lines of arrows. To her great surprise, she noted the paper undulated slightly under her moving finger.

Then she curled up on the carpet beside Arthur and ran her hand along his forearm and smiled as she witnessed the hair moved by the static electricity. She decided to stay close to him during the long night, soaking in his peace, his strength, her mind still racing.

When Arthur awoke seven hours later, Lauren was seated at his worktable.

He rubbed his eyes and gave her a smile she instantly returned.

"You'd have been more comfortable in your bed, but you were sleeping so soundly I didn't dare wake you."

"Did you stay here all night?"

"Yes. You know I like being here with you. It makes me feel more alive."

Arthur was desperate for some coffee and then he'd get right back to work, but she cut him short. "I've given it a lot of thought," she said, and then explained that she was deeply touched by his loyalty, but it was a waste of time. He was not a doctor, she was only a resident, and unaided they had no hope of solving the enigma of the coma.

"Well, do you have any other ideas?"

"I think you should drink your coffee, take a nice

shower, and then come for a stroll with me. You can't live shut away like a hermit in your apartment just because your houseguest is a ghost."

He agreed about the coffee, but he wished she would cut out the "ghost" stuff. She looked like everything you could think of except a ghost. She wanted to know what he meant by "everything," but he refused to be drawn in. "If I say nice things, you'll take advantage of me."

Lauren raised her eyebrows questioningly. "What do you mean by 'nice things'?" He told her just to forget what he had said, but she wouldn't give in. She placed her hands on her hips, planted herself in front of him, and repeated her question.

"I said forget it, Lauren. All I meant is that you're no specter."

"What am I then?"

"A woman, a very beautiful woman. Now I'm taking a shower."

He left the room without looking back. He couldn't deny it, he truly enjoyed her company. She was smart, and funny, and full of life. He knew he was getting in way, way over his head, but he let the shower pound away his doubts and emerged, half an hour later, in jeans and a heavy cashmere sweater. He announced that he felt like eating a good steak.

"It's only ten in the morning," Lauren pointed out.

"But in New York it's lunchtime, and in London it's already time for dinner."

"Yes, but we're not in New York or London."

"That won't change the way my steak tastes."

"I don't know, Arthur, I think it may be time for you to get back to your real life. You're lucky to have one, and I, of all people, know you should live it to the full. You can't just go on dropping everything like this. I can still visit you after work."

"Don't get dramatic on me, Lauren. I'm simply taking a few days off, doing something I want to do."

But she insisted that he was embarking on a dangerous and ultimately pointless course.

He turned on her angrily. "Great! Just great to hear a doctor talk that way. I thought that there was no such thing as a predestined outcome, that anything is possible. Why do I have greater faith than you?"

Precisely because she was a doctor, she said, because she believed she saw things clearly, because she saw that they were wasting their time, his time. "You shouldn't get attached to me, I have nothing to offer you, nothing to share, nothing to give! I can't even make you a cup of coffee!"

"Shit. If you can't make me a cup of coffee, then there's really no hope at all for the future." Arthur paused. "I'm not doing this only for you, Lauren. I'm doing it for me too. I didn't ask to find you in my closet, only there you were! And I'm the only one who can help you, and it's the right thing to do. The only thing to do. That's life, that's just how things are. No one but me can hear you or see you or talk to you. I can't abandon you now."

She was right, he went on, to say that what they were doing was fraught with risk. "For both of us," he said. "For you, because maybe we are really wasting our time, maybe there really is nothing we can do to help you get back into your body. And I'll admit, I'm turning my life upside down a bit—but that's just my point—that's life." He had no choice. She was in a difficult situation and he was taking care of her: "That's what people do in a civilized world, never mind the risks involved." As he saw it, giving a dollar to a homeless man outside the supermarket was easy; it cost you nothing. "It's when you give something you have very little of that you truly give. Look, I know you don't really know that much about me, but you must believe that I feel right about what I'm doing—believe me the way I believed you.

"You have to allow me to help you," he continued. "In fact your willingness to accept my help is about all you still possess of real life. If you think I'm doing this without taking the time to really think it through, you're absolutely right. It would take me the rest of my life to think *this* through. Because it's while you're thinking, while you're sweating things out, while you're weighing the pros and cons, that life goes on—passes you by while you're doing nothing. I don't know how, but we're going to get you out of this. If you were meant to die, you'd already be dead. I'm just here to give you a hand."

He concluded by asking her to accept what he was doing, if not for herself then at least for all the people she'd be taking care of in a few years' time.

"You could have been a lawyer," Lauren said, shaking her head.

"I should have been a doctor."

"Why didn't you become one?"

"Because my mom died too early."

"How old were you?"

"Much too young," he said quietly. "Let's drop the subject, okay?"

"It might help to talk about it. . . ."

He pointed out that she was a physician, not a psychiatrist. He didn't want to talk about his mother's death because it was too painful to dwell on it. He had lost his mother when he was very young, and his father even earlier. "The past is the past, end of story." He paused. "So, I'm not a doctor; instead I run an architectural firm. I like what I do and the people I work with." Lauren waited for him to continue. "Look, I'm still very hungry, so even if this isn't London, and I can't get a steak, I'm still going to make myself eggs and bacon."

She followed him into the kitchen.

"Who took care of you after your parents died?"

"You don't take no for an answer, do you?"

"Not a chance. I want to know what happened in your life to make you capable of this."

"Capable of what?"

"Of dropping everything to take care of the shadow of a woman you don't know—and you don't even have a shot at getting in my pants—since I don't even have any. So I'm curious."

"Listen, I'm not hiding anything, okay? I simply have a past that couldn't be more concrete or more complete—because it's the past, it's over."

"So I have no right to get to know you?"

"Of course you have the right, but what you're asking about right now is my past, it's not me."

"You're right. You're the only person whose past has absolutely no influence whatsoever on who you are," she said.

"Now who should have been the lawyer!"

"Yes, but I'm a doctor."

Without a word, Arthur rose and took his plate to the kitchen. Lauren stayed in the living room, quietly taking in what he'd told her. In a few minutes, Arthur returned to his desk.

"Have you loved many women?" she asked him softly, without looking up.

"Who counts when you're in love!"

"And have there been many who 'counted'?"

He told that he had had three loves: one as a teenager, one as a young man, and one as a "not-so-young man." That struck her as a fair answer, but she at once wanted to know why it hadn't worked out with Carol Ann. He thought it was because he was too complete. "You mean possessive?" she asked.

"No, I mean complete. My mother filled me with stories about ideal love. . . . Having such ideals is a heavy burden, at times."

"Why?"

"I set my standards much too high."

"For your women?"

"No, for myself."

She asked him to elaborate, but he refused: he did not want to seem "old-fashioned and ridiculous." She told him to try anyway. Knowing he had no chance of deflecting her from the subject, he said, "Recognizing happiness when it's lying at your feet, having the will and the courage to reach down and take it in your arms . . . and to hold on to it. That's the heart's intelligence. Intelligence minus heart is just logic—which doesn't amount to much."

"So Carol Ann left you!"

Arthur did not reply.

"And you haven't quite healed?"

"Oh, I've healed all right; perhaps the problem was I was never sick."

"You couldn't love her?"

"Everyone is scared that by sharing everyday life with

someone, they're going to get bored and caught up in routines, but I don't believe that has to be inevitable."

"What do you believe, then?"

"I believe that everyday life with someone is the ground in which true intimacy grows. Far from creating a rut, I believe it gives you a shot at reinventing life, the whole spectrum, from the sublime to the ridiculous."

For him there was nothing more complete than time-tested love, a couple journeying together and welcoming the gradual evolution of passion into tenderness. But how could you ever know what that was like if you kept aspiring to an absolute? As he saw it, there was nothing wrong with keeping some of the child in yourself alive, your share of youthful dreams.

"Is this something you know from experience?"

"Not really. I wish!" He hesitated. "What about you? Have you ever been in love?"

"Do you know many people who haven't been in love? You want to know if I love anyone? No; well, yes and no."

"Who was he?"

"He still is: thirty-eight, movie director, good-looking, hard to pin down, a bit selfish, the ideal man . . ."

"And so?"

"It was thousands of light-years away from the sort of love you're talking about."

"Tell me about him."

She had shared four years of her life with her film director, four years of a stormy on-again, off-again drama in which the actors tore one another to pieces then glued themselves back again time after time, as if histrionics added another dimension to life. She said it was a selfish relationship kept alive mostly by physical passion.

"Are you very physical?"

She found the question rather funny, under the circumstances.

"You don't have to answer."

"And I don't intend to! Anyway, he broke it off six
months before the accident. Good for him. At least he needn't
feel any sense of obligation toward me today."

"Do you miss him?"

"I missed him when we first broke up."

Some people might lose their ideals as they age, but with
Lauren it was the opposite. The older she got, the more ide-
alistic she became.

"I think that couples shouldn't even contemplate living together unless they are truly ready to give. Unless you have
that degree of commitment, you're only fooling yourself if
you think your relationship has meaning. Happiness is not
just there for the taking. You're either a giver or a receiver. I
give before I receive, but I'm definitely done with selfish people, complicated people and people who are too stingy to give
themselves a chance to fulfill their hopes and dreams." There
comes a time, she said, when we have to take honest stock of
ourselves and identify what it is we really want out of life.

Arthur thought she was taking things much too seriously. "I've been attracted to the opposite of my ideal man
for too long. Men at the opposite extreme from what would
make me happy, that's all," she replied. Arthur took Lauren's hand. "Come on, lets get some fresh air."

They drove in silence all the way to Ocean Beach, Arthur
lost in his thoughts, Lauren in hers. It had been a long
morning.

When they parked, Arthur went around and opened the
door for Lauren. He bowed as she got out of the car and

took her hand. "I like being by the water," he said to break the silence.

Lauren did not answer at once; she was gazing at the horizon. She put her hand on Arthur's arm.

"You're not like other men."

"Is it my two noses that bother you?"

"Nothing bothers me. But you're different from the other men I've known."

"Really? In what way?"

"You're less obvious."

"Is that a fault?"

"No, but it's unusual. Nothing seems to be a problem for you."

"I don't mind problems, because I like finding solutions."

"There's more to it than that."

"Here she is again, my PPS!"

"What's a PPS?"

"My personal portable shrink."

"I have nothing to hide, Lauren, no dark side, no twilight zone, no secrets. I am who I am, and believe me, my shortcomings are many." He was glad he had never felt bound by conformity. Perhaps that was what she sensed. "I'm not part of any system, I've always fought that. I see the people I like, I go where I want, I read a book because it interests me and not because it's on the best-seller list. My whole life has been that way. I don't burden myself with overanalyzing everything."

The conversation resumed after they had gone inside to the welcome warmth of a hotel. Arthur was drinking a cappuccino and munching on cookies.

"I love this place," he said, his eyes scanning the room.

On a couch sat a small boy of seven or eight, curled up in

his mother's arms. She held a big, open book and was describing the pictures on each page. Her left index finger stroked the child's cheek slowly and tenderly. His two dimples, like tiny suns, gave him a radiant smile. Arthur watched them for a long time.

"What are you looking at?" asked Lauren.

"That kid over there. Look at his face, he's deep in his own world."

"Does that bring back memories?"

He merely smiled.

"You and your mother must have been very close."

"The most amazing thing about the day my mother left was that all the buildings were still there, the streets were full of cars whose wheels went on rolling, and pedestrians went on walking, apparently unaware that my own world had just vanished. When I was in my mother's arms, nothing could bother me, not big Steve Hachenbach the school bully, not Mr. Morton yelling at me for not finishing my homework, not the rancid smell of the cafeteria. I'll tell you why I'm 'less obvious,' as you call it. My mother taught me to focus on what's essential, and not to get caught up in the rest."

"I hope Providence is listening on my behalf; my 'essential' is still ahead of me."

"That's why it's 'essential' for us not to give up." He rose. "C'mon, let's go home and get back to work."

Arthur paid the check and they walked to the parking lot. Before he got back in the car, Lauren kissed him on the cheek. "Thanks for everything," she said. Arthur smiled and blushed.

Eight

ARTHUR SPENT MOST OF THE NEXT TWO WEEKS IN THE city library, an imposing turn-of-the-century building in the neoclassical style. There were dozens of reading rooms with lofty vaulted ceilings. The medical books were kept in Room 27. Arthur sat in Row 48, the one closest to the neurology section. There he scanned thousands of pages on coma, unconsciousness, and cranial trauma. Although the texts gave him a clearer understanding of Lauren's problem, they brought him no closer to figuring out how to help her get back in her body. After his reading, he spent a day E-mailing eminent professors of medicine and well-known research doctors, describing his dilemma, pretending he was working on a novel. Some of them answered, perhaps intrigued by the purpose of his research. They all agreed— the situation he described was medically impossible, and if it ever were possible, he would need a shaman or a priest or a psychic, rather than a scientist, to solve his problem.

Each afternoon he called Paul to keep up with details at the office and to reassure him that he hadn't yet had a nervous breakdown or a massive stroke. He was learning a lot about himself, and about ghosts, he told Paul, with a chuckle.

Paul seemed to take these reassurances at face value. "Just do what you need to do, buddy, I'm holding down the fort at this end. But I miss you. Let me know when you want to get together."

Each evening Arthur returned to find Lauren waiting for him. He'd make himself dinner and tell her about the day's research, trying to put the most positive spin on it he could.

Lauren was amazed by how quickly he had acquired a medical vocabulary, but to what purpose? "I'm afraid we're getting nowhere, Arthur," she said when he returned on the fourth night.

"I've got another idea, though," he reassured her. "From the brain of no less than your colleague the eminent Dr. Weltnung. 'Look to the mystic,' he told me, 'that's your hope.' "

"Oh, spare me," Lauren moaned. "Arthur, you're getting desperate. You can't believe you can find anything there."

Arguments and counterarguments ensued, deep into the night and past the point of exhaustion. Finally Arthur retreated to his bedroom.

Lauren listened to the lonely night sounds, watching the hours click by, the darkness ever so gradually giving way to dawn. She worried all night, thinking about Arthur. She couldn't go on letting him pursue this wild-goose chase— especially since the goose had just become quite a bit wilder. But by the next morning, when she heard Arthur stirring in the bedroom, she realized she wouldn't try to stop him in his paranormal researches. This was about something beyond medicine, or it had become about something beyond that. It was about life, and love, and the meaning of both. And even a skeptical scientist such as herself knew that the metaphysical, spiritual branches of knowledge, although she still had trouble calling it that, were better at dealing with those questions.

As Arthur ate his breakfast that day, he outlined for her the new track he would follow during the coming day's research. "Let me come with you," she said. "Let me read over your shoulder. If you're going into this sort of inquiry, I think I better be there with you."

He refused to let her come with him. "Your presence would distract me," he said, hiding a blush. "Besides, I think it's time for you to spend more of your days at the hospital. Try a bit harder to get into your body." He stopped, realizing he'd made an awkward pun. "Well, you know what I mean. Maybe if you concentrate more, focus bone by bone, muscle by muscle, tendon by tendon—you know, the way they do in the yoga classes—maybe you can bring it back. In the meantime, I'll go on the treasure hunt and see if I can find some arcane key to your reunion with your body."

After days of reading just about every quack on the shelves who had something to say about astral projection or life after death, Arthur decided they needed a change of pace. A smile formed on his lips as he abruptly swung into California Street and stopped at the gourmet supermarket. He hadn't found an answer, he had nothing to be joyous about, yet he had the urge to celebrate. Even in the face of this impossible, ridiculous situation, he felt light, energized. Preposterous as it seemed, Lauren was real to him, realer than any other woman he'd ever known. And if he was mad, crazy, off his rocker, so be it. But tonight he would go home and decorate the table with candles and roses, flood the apartment with Barry White music, and ask Lauren to dance.

The Bay glowed with a splendid sunset as he parked the car. He skipped up the stairs, performed a balancing act to get the key in the lock, and went inside, arms loaded with packages. He pushed the door shut with his foot and set the bags down on the kitchen counter.

Lauren was sitting on the window seat in the living room, contemplating the view. She did not rise to greet him, as she usually did, or even turn around to look at him.

"Hey, what's wrong?" Arthur asked as he walked over to her. As he reached down to put a hand on her shoulder, she suddenly disappeared. Arthur heard her grumbling from the bedroom, "Jesus, I can't even slam a door!"

"Did something happen?" he called after her.

"Leave me alone!"

Arthur took off his coat and went to the bedroom. When he opened the door, he saw Lauren leaning against the window, her head in her hands. Her shoulders shook as if she were sobbing.

"Are you crying?"

"I have no tears, how can I cry?"

"You're sobbing! What's going on?"

He wanted to look her in the eye, but she turned her back. "Leave me alone. Please, just leave me."

Arthur placed his hands on her shoulders and turned her around to face him. He raised her lowered head with the tip of his finger and looked in her ever-changing eyes. "Tell me what's wrong."

"They're going to end it."

"Who's going to end what?"

"I went to the hospital this morning. Mom was there, talking to me. It seems she's been having meetings for the past week with the ethical committee. They've decided it's time to remove my feeding tube."

"What does this mean?"

"It means I'm going to die."

The hospital's ethics committee and right-to-die counselors had contacted Lauren's mother several times over the past few weeks, but not until last week had she been ready to meet with them. Yesterday, as she did every morning, she had gone to Memorial Hospital, then met with the specialists who handled issues of dying and artificial life support. An older woman, Dr. Clomb, a psychiatrist, had led the discussion. According to the story Mrs. Kline recounted to Lauren's lifeless body, Dr. Clomb had launched into yet another long monologue designed to convince Mrs. Kline to accept the inevitable. Lauren was no longer anything but a body without a soul, being kept alive at an exorbitant cost to society. It was easier on the family to keep a loved one artificially alive than to decide to accept death, but at what price? Mrs. Kline had to accept the unacceptable and steel herself to it. The case was hopeless. They all had to have the courage to admit it. Dr. Clomb emphasized that the mother was developing a state of emotional "dependency" on her daughter's body. The doctor's logic, well polished over time, progressively chiseled away at Mrs. Kline's emotional resistance to the "rational and humane" decision. With practiced, subtle logic, Dr. Clomb argued that to refuse would be unjust, cruel, both for the patient and her mother: cruel—selfish—unhealthy. The psychiatrist spoke with great tact and delicacy. And now doubt was gaining ground. Lauren could only listen helplessly as her mother told her lifeless body the whole story. Lauren watched her mother weep as she talked of the torment she'd been through for the past months, of her uncertainty of what the right thing to do was. After what felt like the longest hours of her life, Mrs. Kline broke. In tears, she told her daughter that she had decided that she needed to let Lauren go, let her die, that she needed to set her body free. "So, Lauren, my beloved daughter," she said through her tears, "after all these years, I, who gave you life, am going to allow you to die. I've forced you to stay alive too long now, I've been selfish, not wanting to let you go. But I know it's time. I'm going to wait over the weekend, to make sure, but next Monday, I'll meet with the doctors and sign the papers. If you're in there, Lauren, in there anywhere, please give me a sign, let me know if I've made the wrong decision." Her mother knelt before the bed and placed her hands on Lauren's lifeless ones. Lauren tried with every fiber of whatever it was she was now to give her mother a sign, to move merely a finger, a toe, but to no avail. Finally, after two hours of pure frustration and terror, Lauren left her mother and her own body, leaving the two of them together.

Lauren bowed her head. "I came straight back here to the window seat. I want to soak in all the lights, all the views, all the smells, and all the excitement of the city while there's still time. Today's Thursday. I have only a few more days to live."

Arthur took her in his arms, enveloping her in tenderness. "I won't let them do it."

"How will you stop them?"

"Give me a couple of hours to think about it."

She floated out of his arms and turned back to the window. "What's the point?" she said, staring at the streetlamp below. "Maybe it's for the best; maybe they're right."

"What do you mean, 'it's for the best'?"

Lauren, normally so strong, so determined, seemed to have resigned herself. "In truth, all I have left is a half life. Besides, I'm ruining my mother's life and yours."

"How can you think even for a moment that your mother would be relieved if you die for good?"

Lauren couldn't help but smile. "Thanks for that."

"What did I say?"

"It's just the expression 'die for good.' Under the circumstances, you know."

"Do you believe your mom could ever fill the empty space you'd leave behind? Do you truly think it's best for her if you give up? And what about me?"

She looked at him inquiringly. "What about you?"

"I'll be there when you wake up. You may be invisible to other people, but not to me."

"Is that a declaration?"

Now she was mocking him. "Don't be so full of yourself," he said dryly.

"Why are you hanging around me, making plans, fighting on my behalf? What's gone wrong in that brain of yours?" Now she was practically screaming. "What's your motive?"

"You know what my motive is, Lauren."

Lauren said nothing, muttering something inaudible.

"I need to try and talk to your mother," Arthur said after a long pause. "I think that's our best hope. I somehow need to persuade her not to let them take out your feeding tube."

At first Lauren said that would be impossible, but after another half hour of arguing, she modified her assessment to difficult. "You've never met my mom. She's a very private

person, and now she's practically sick with grief. I'm the
only family she has. I don't know how we can engineer a
meeting." Lauren thought some more. "Mom would never
just invite you in to have a talk about letting her daughter
die—not unless you have some way of getting some professional credentials, and even then, I think she's had enough
of such discussions at this point."

"What if I ran into her by chance?"

"But how would you introduce the subject of me? You
can't just walk up to her and say, 'Hi, you don't know me,
but I'm here to tell you your daughter's alive and well as a
ghost in my apartment!'"

They stared at each other for a long time, then fell silent,
both lost in thought.

"Wait. I got it," Lauren said excitedly. "She walks the
dog on the Marina every morning."

"Yes, but then I'd have to have a dog to walk too."

"Why?"

"Because if I take a leash for a walk with no dog on the
other end, my credibility would be shot."

"Ha, ha, ha. Then just go jogging."

He liked the idea. He could time his run to coincide with
Kali's walk. After he made a fuss over the dog, it would be
easy to strike up a conversation with Lauren's mother.

Nine

Early the next morning he put on sweatpants and a sweatshirt. Before leaving, he asked Lauren to hold him tight in her arms.

"What's with you today?" she asked shyly.

"Nothing. I don't have time to explain. It's for the dog."

She complied, laying her head on his shoulder.

"That's fine," he said briskly, and pulled away. "Now I'm off, otherwise I'll miss her."

Without even saying good-bye, he rushed out of the apartment. The door closed. Lauren shrugged and sighed, "He hugged me because of the dog."

The Golden Gate was still sleeping under a blanket of fog when Arthur arrived. Only the pinnacles of the red bridge emerged from the mist. The sea was calm in the prison of the Bay, the early-morning gulls making wide, circular sweeps in their quest for fish. The sprawling lawns bordering the wharves were still soaked in the night's sea spray, and the moored boats bobbed gently on the water. Everything was peaceful; a few early joggers cut through the foggy air. In a few hours, a fat sun would crest the heights of Sausalito and Tiburon and free the red bridge from its shroud.

Arthur spotted Lauren's mother from a long way off, matching perfectly the description her daughter had given him.

Kali trotted a few steps ahead of Mrs. Kline, who, lost in thought, seemed to be carrying the weight of the world on her shoulders. Approaching Arthur, Kali suddenly stopped short, sniffing the air with a circling movement of her muzzle and head. She came closer, sniffing the bottom of Arthur's leg, and then she lay down at his feet, whimpering, her tail thumping the ground. Kali was trembling with joy and excitement. Arthur knelt down and began to stroke her gently. The dog licked his hand, her plaintive whines growing louder and more urgent.

Lauren's mother drew near, looking greatly surprised. "Do you know each other?"

"Why do you ask?" Arthur said as he rose.

"She's usually so fearful, nobody can get close to her. But she's falling all over you."

"She looks unbelievably like the dog of a friend who was very dear to me."

"Yes?" said Mrs. Kline, her heart beginning to race.

The dog sat up and began to yap, holding out her paw to Arthur. "Kali!" exclaimed Lauren's mother. "Leave the gentleman alone."

Arthur stuck out his hand and introduced himself. "I know Kali, of course, she's Lauren's dog!"

After a moment's hesitation Mrs. Kline took his hand but

did not introduce herself. She was disturbed by her dog's behavior, and she apologized to Arthur for Kali's excess of familiarity.

"No problem."

Then Mrs. Kline suddenly fell silent, looking like a statue of despair.

"Are you all right, ma'am?" asked Arthur, taking her hand.

"You know my daughter?"

"Yes, I know her very well. We were quite close."

She told him she had never heard Lauren mention him and asked how he and Lauren had met. He told her he was an architect. He had met Lauren at the hospital when she stitched up his hand after an accident with a paper cutter. They had hit it off and saw each other fairly often. "Every now and then I dropped by and had lunch with her at the hospital, and we sometimes met for dinner when she finished early."

"Lauren never had time for lunch, and she always got home late," her mother said suspiciously.

Arthur lowered his head and said nothing.

"But Kali does seem to know you."

"I know this must be hard for you, and I'm more sorry than I can say about what happened to Lauren, ma'am. I've visited her at the hospital several times."

"I've never seen you there."

He asked if he could stroll with her a little. They walked by the water. Arthur ventured to ask for news about Lauren's condition, explaining that he had not been able to see her for some time. Mrs. Kline told him the situation had not improved, that there was no longer any hope. She said nothing of the decision she had reached, but she described her daughter's condition in resolutely bleak terms.

After a few moments' silence, Arthur began to plead for continued faith. "Doctors don't know everything about comas. Some patients have come back after years. . . . And miracles do happen, I read about it all the time. Nothing is more sacred than life, and when, against all odds, it persists, it's a sign that should not be ignored." He even invoked God, as "the only one with the right to dispense life and death."

Mrs. Kline suddenly stopped walking and looked Arthur straight in the eyes. "You didn't just run into me now by accident, did you? Who are you and what do you want?"

"I was just out running, ma'am, and if you believe this wasn't just a chance meeting, you have to ask yourself why. I didn't teach Lauren's dog to come to me without being called."

"What do you want from me? And what right do you have to preach to me about life and death? You don't know how it feels to be there every day, to see her lying there, inert, unresponsive, not moving even an eyelash, to see her chest rising and falling but her face closed to the world."

In a burst of anger, she told him about the days and nights she had spent talking to Lauren in the vain hope that Lauren might hear. Her life had ended with her daughter's accident, leaving her an empty existence waiting for a call from the hospital to say it was all over.

"Every day of my life I wake up thinking of her, go to bed thinking of her . . ." Mrs. Kline broke off and began to weep. Arthur put his hand on her shoulder and said he was sorry.

"I can't go on," she muttered. "I'm sorry. Please leave me; I should never have spoken to you."

Arthur apologized again, patted the dog's head, and walked slowly away. He got into his car, and as he drove away, he saw Lauren's mother in the rearview mirror, watching him leave.

When he reached his apartment, Lauren was balancing on the edge of the coffee table.

"What are you doing?" he asked.

"Practicing."

"I see."

"How did it go?"

He gave her a detailed account of the meeting and said how disappointed he was at his failure to sway her mother.

"You never had much of a chance, really. She never changes her mind, especially if it's a decision she's taken a long, hard time to come to. She's stubborn as a mule."

"Don't be hard on her, she's going through hell."

"What a son-in-law you would make! You're just the kind of guy mothers adore."

"That's a bit beside the point, isn't it?"

"I just thought of a good one: if you married me, you'd be a widower before you even had a wife."

"Is that a proposal?"

"No. Forget I spoke." Lauren looked depressed. "This has been a really bad morning. I need to be alone." With that, she disappeared.

When she returned that evening, she found Arthur at his desk, making a long list on a legal pad.

"What kind of treatment do they give your body at the hospital?" Arthur asked her as soon as he realized she was back.

"You mean aside from hygiene?"

"I mean the medical care."

She told him that she was fed through the feeding tube, three times a day. Three times a week, antibiotics were injected into the drip feed as a precautionary measure. She described how she was turned over every morning and every night, the massages administered to her hips, elbows, knees, and shoulders to maintain joint mobility. It was mostly simple nursing care, simple physical care, to try to prevent her body from further curling in on itself, and to minimize bedsores. The rest of the treatment consisted of monitoring her vital signs and temperature.

"My heart and lungs function on their own, so I'm breathing on my own. That's their whole problem. Otherwise they could simply pull the plug."

"Have you ever looked after patients in your condition?"

She had cared for patients admitted to the emergency room, but only for short spells, until a room was found for them, never on a prolonged basis. "But if you *had* to?" She supposed that she could handle it. For the most part, skilled nursing care was all that was required, except in the event of sudden complications.

"So you'd know what to do?"

"I guess so. What are you getting at?"

"Is the feeding a problem?" he asked.

"In what way?"

"Hard to get hold of. Is it available in a pharmacy?"

"At the hospital pharmacy, yes."

"And in a public pharmacy?"

She thought for a few seconds, then nodded. The drip feed could be reconstituted by buying glucose, anticoagulants, saline, and so forth and blending them together, and they just used something like Ensure for the feeding tube. It was feasible. Besides, people on home care had their IV fluids and food administered by nurses, who ordered the products from a central pharmacy.

"I have to bring Paul into this," Arthur said.

"What for?"

"For the ambulance."

"The ambulance? What are you planning?"

"We're going to kidnap you."

"What?" Now she was getting worried.

"We're going to kidnap you. So they can't stop feeding you."

"You're out of your mind!"

"Not completely."

"How can we kidnap me? Where will we hide the body? Who'll take care of it?"

"One question at a time!"

She would take care of the body, or she'd teach him how to; she had the necessary experience. They just had to obtain the fluids necessary for the IV, but according to her that should not be too difficult.

"Who will write the prescriptions?" she asked.

"That takes us back to your first question: How?"

"And?"

"Paul's stepfather runs an auto-body shop; they specialize in rescue vehicles brought in by firefighters, police, EMS. We can 'borrow' an ambulance. It can't be that hard. We'll get our hands on a pair of white scrub suits and take you out of the hospital."

Lauren gave a nervous laugh. "Wait a minute. It's not that simple!"

She reminded him that entering a hospital was not like entering a supermarket. Getting out of one was even more complicated. To move a patient involved a number of administrative steps. First, one needed a certificate of admission from the facility that would be receiving the patient.

Other necessary documents included an authorization for the patient's transfer signed by the doctor, a voucher from the ambulance company, and a statement regarding the patient's condition and the patient's requirements during transportation.

"That's where you come in, Lauren, you're going to help me get all that paperwork."

"But I can't carry anything, let alone pick anything up."

"But you know where the forms are kept."

"Yes. So?"

"So I'm the one who'll steal them. Are you familiar with what they look like?"

"Of course. I often arranged transfers." She went on to describe them as just typical forms, printed on white, pink, and blue paper, with the hospital's or the ambulance service's letterhead.

"We'll get our hands on some and forge them," he said excitedly. "Come on, let's go."

Arthur grabbed his jacket and keys and ordered Lauren to follow him in a tone that allowed her no leeway to oppose his far-fetched plan. They got in the car and drove out onto Green Street. He drove fast to Memorial Hospital and headed straight for the emergency-services parking lot. When Lauren asked what he was going to do, he replied with a faint smile at the corners of his mouth, "Follow me and keep a straight face!"

As he was going through the first door of the emergency bay, Arthur bent over double and groped his way to the reception desk. The nurse on duty asked him what was wrong. He described violent cramps that had set in two hours after dinner. To make sure he didn't get whisked to the operating room, he mentioned twice that he'd already had his appendix out. A nurse gave him a clipboard with forms to fill out, then led him to an examination cubicle where she took his blood pressure and temperature. Then she left, saying that the doctor would be in shortly. Lauren, perched on the arm of a wheelchair, was beginning to smile broadly. Arthur was playing his part perfectly. Even she had been worried when he had first collapsed on entering the waiting room.

"You don't know what you're getting yourself into," she murmured as a doctor came in to examine him.

Dr. Spacek introduced himself and drew the curtain around the cubicle. He had Arthur lie down on the examination table and asked him about his symptoms while scanning Arthur's file. Other than for the age at which he had entered puberty, he had written down his entire medical and personal history, as detailed as a coroner's inquest. Arthur said he suffered from terrible cramps.

"Can you point to where it hurts the most?" asked the doctor.

"No, it's everywhere, all over my stomach; I feel as sick as a dog."

"Don't lay it on so thick," whispered Lauren, "or else he'll give you a shot of tranquilizers, have you spend the night here, and tomorrow morning you'll get a barium enema, followed by a fibroscopy and a colonoscopy."

"No shots!" Arthur blurted out.

"I didn't say anything about shots," observed Dr. Spacek, looking up from his folder.

"No, but I'd just as soon say so right away because I hate shots."

The doctor asked him whether he was nervous by nature, and Arthur nodded.

"Now I'm going to palpate your abdomen to find out

where the pain is sharpest." Arthur nodded again. The doctor placed his hands one on top of the other and began to press on every inch of Arthur's abdomen.

"Does it hurt here?"

"Uh, yes," he said hesitantly.

"Here?"

"No, you're not supposed to hurt there," whispered Lauren with a smile, and Arthur at once denied any discomfort.

Lauren continued to guide Arthur throughout the examination. The doctor diagnosed spasms of the colon due to nerves and handed Arthur a prescription for an antispasmodic medication. Two handshakes and three "Thank you, Doctor's" later, Arthur was striding down the long corridor that led to the exit. In his hand he had three different forms, all with Memorial Hospital's letterhead and logo. One blue, one pink, one green. One was a prescription, one was a receipt itemizing services and charges, and the third was a disposition form headed, in large capitals, AUTHORIZA-TION FOR TRANSFER / AUTHORIZATION FOR DIS-CHARGE, noting below that, in italics, *Circle the one that is applicable*. He wore a broad grin of self-satisfaction. Lauren walked beside him. He put his arm around her. "We make a pretty good team, don't we?"

Back at the apartment, he slipped the three documents into his computer scanner and copied them. Now he possessed an unlimited source of printed forms of every shape and color with the official imprimatur of Memorial.

"You're very good," said Lauren as the first official-looking forms emerged from the color printer.

"In an hour or so I'll call Paul."

"Can we please discuss your plans first."

"You're right. I need to quiz you more about this whole procedure of transferring a patient."

But that was not what she wanted to discuss. "Arthur, God knows I'm moved by your project. But, let's face it, it's unrealistic, crazy, and much too dangerous for you. You'll go to jail if you're caught."

"Jail doesn't compare to what you risk if we don't try anything. We only have two full days, Lauren. I don't have any choice."

"You can't do it Arthur, I don't have the right to let you go ahead. Sorry."

"I once knew a girl who said sorry whenever she opened her mouth. It got to the point where her friends were too scared to offer her a glass of water, for fear she'd apologize for being thirsty."

"Arthur, don't kid around. It's a crazy plan."

"It's the situation that's crazy, Lauren. Please help. We're wasting valuable time. It's your life that's at stake."

There was no alternative, and it was vital to move quickly. On Monday, the doctors would be removing her feeding tube. Arthur made a list of the accessories he would need to put his plan into action. He printed his document and picked up the phone to call Paul.

"I have to see you as soon as possible. It's urgent, Paul, I need you."

"Where do you want to meet?"

"Wherever you like."

"Come to my place."

Half an hour later Paul let him in. They sat on couches in the living room.

"What's up?"

"I need you to do me a favor with no questions asked. I want you to help me kidnap a body from the hospital."

"What's the deal? You're through with the ghost, and now you want a corpse? I can give you mine if you keep this up. It'll be up for grabs pretty soon at this rate!"

"It isn't a corpse."

"What is it then? A hospital patient in the peak of health?"

"I'm serious, Paul, and in a hurry."

"I'm not allowed to ask questions?"

"You'd have a hard time understanding the answers."

"Because I'm too dumb?"

"Because no one could believe what I'm going through."

"Try me."

"I want you to help me remove the body of a woman in a coma. They're going to terminate her on Monday. And I'm not going to let them."

"You've fallen in love with a woman in a coma? Is that what that ghost business was all about?"

Arthur mumbled a vague "Uh-huh."

Paul, who had been leaning forward alertly, fell back on the couch and sighed deeply. "This is going to cost you a couple of thousand hours with a shrink. Listen, I've gone along with you for almost two weeks, Arthur. But I'm your friend, and I have a responsibility to stop you from doing something crazy. Have you really thought this through? Your mind's made up?"

"With or without you, I'm going to do it."

"You really love to keep things simple, don't you?"

"If you don't want to get involved, just say so."

"Let's see if I have it straight. You show up looking like hell and ask me to risk ten years in the slammer to help you lift a body from a hospital. I think I'll just pray to be transformed into the Dalai Lama, it's my only chance. . . . So, what exactly do you need from me?"

Arthur explained his plan, and what he needed from Paul: basically an ambulance. They could borrow one from Paul's stepfather's body shop.

"Oh, it gets even better! Now I get to rob my mother's husband! It's good to know you, pal, my life would never have been the same without you."

"I know I'm asking a lot. But I swear on my mother's grave, Paul, I have to do this. I have to do this more than I've ever had to do anything in my life."

That got Paul's attention. He knew Arthur would never invoke his mother's name except in matters of life and death. "Okay, when do you need it?"

Arthur wanted to have the ambulance on Sunday night. The best time to steal the body was at 11 P.M., when the staff was changing shifts. Paul should pick him up in the ambulance at half past ten. Arthur would call him again early tomorrow morning to fine-tune the details. Arthur hugged his friend hard. Looking preoccupied, Paul walked Arthur to his car.

"Thank you," said Arthur through the window.

"That's what friends are for. At the end of the month I may ask you to help me climb a mountain to give a manicure to a grizzly bear. Go on, get out of here, you look as though you've lots more to do."

As the car crossed the intersection and disappeared, Paul raised his arms heavenward and shouted, "Why me?" He waited for several moments, and when it seemed clear that no answer was forthcoming, he shrugged and muttered, "Yeah, I know, I know. *Why not?*"

The next day, Arthur raced from pharmacy to pharmacy,

loading his car trunk with medical supplies. Back in the apartment, he found Lauren resting on his bed. He sat down carefully beside her and ran his hand just above her hair, not touching it. Then he whispered, "You know, you're really very beautiful." He left just as quietly as he had entered and went back to his architect's table in the living room. As soon as he was out of the room, Lauren opened her eyes and smiled.

In the living room, Arthur picked up the administrative forms he had printed the day before and began filling them in, leaving an occasional blank. Then he put everything in a folder. He took the folder, put on his jacket, went down to the car and drove to the hospital. He parked in the lot by the emergency entrance and moved stealthily through the automatic doors. He turned and headed for the staff lounge. A nurse taking a break there addressed him, "Excuse me, can I help you?"

He explained that he was springing a surprise on an old friend who worked here. "Perhaps you know her; her name is Lauren Kline."

The nurse fell silent, and it took her a moment to find her words. "When did you see her last?"

"Oh, last summer." On the spur of the moment he improvised that he was a photojournalist just back from Africa, and Lauren was his cousin by marriage. "Doesn't she work here anymore?"

The nurse said he would have to ask at the information desk next to admissions in the main hospital. She was sorry, but Lauren was not here in this department.

Arthur put on an anxious face and asked whether there was some kind of problem. Clearly ill at ease, the nurse again told him the information desk should be able to help him. Not the ER reception desk, she added, but the one in the main hospital.

"Do I have to leave the building to get there?"

"In theory, yes. You're supposed to go back out and go around."

Instead, she told him how he could take a shortcut through the building to the hospital lobby. Carefully maintaining his anxious expression, he thanked her and said good-bye. Once out of the nurse's sight, he slipped from corridor to corridor until he found what he was looking for. Through a half-open door he spied two white coats on hangers. He went in, snatched them down, and bundled them under his coat. In the pocket of one he felt a stethoscope. Then he was out in the corridor again, following the nurse's directions until he emerged from the main hospital entrance. He walked around the building, found his car in the emergency parking lot, and went home.

Lauren was seated at his desk, reading the details of his plan. Before he was across the threshold, she exclaimed, "You're out of your mind!" Without replying, he showed her the two white coats.

"I suppose you have an ambulance in the garage?"

"Paul's in charge of the ambulance. He'll have it when he picks me up at ten-thirty tomorrow night."

"Where did you get the coats?"

"At your hospital."

"Is there anything that can stop you once you've made up your mind to do something? Show me the name tags."

Arthur put on one of the lab coats, took a few steps, and turned, like a fashion model on a runway.

"What do you think?"

"You've stolen Bronswick's coat!"

"Who's he?"

"A well-known cardiologist. There's going to be hell to pay at the hospital when he notices it's missing. I can just imagine the flurry of memos. Security's going to get an earful. Bronswick is the most arrogant and foul-tempered medic in the whole hospital."

"What are the chances of someone realizing I'm not Bronswick?"

She told him not to worry. The risk was small; it would take really bad luck. Bronswick was normally around in the daytime on weekdays. The night-shift staff and the weekend personnel probably didn't know him by sight. Arthur wasn't likely to encounter a member of Bronswick's team. On Sunday night, it would be a different hospital, with different people and a different atmosphere.

"And look, I even have a stethoscope!"

"Hang it around your neck."

He did so.

"You know what? You make a terribly sexy doctor," she said, her voice soft and very feminine.

Arthur looked down at his feet. She took his hand and stroked his fingers and said in the same sweet voice, "Thank you for all you're doing for me. No one has ever taken care of me like this."

"Superman . . . to the rescue, Lois," he said, pulling away.

They looked into each other's eyes. He took her in his arms, placed his hand on the back of her neck, and brought her head to rest on his shoulder. "We have a lot to do," he told her. "I have to get back to work."

He returned to his desk. Lauren looked at him intently and then silently withdrew to the bedroom, leaving the door open. He worked late into the night, stopping only for a light snack. He concentrated on his notes as he typed out line after line of text on his screen. He heard the television go on. "How did you do that?" he called out. She did not reply. He stood up, crossed the living room, and peeked through the doorway. Lauren was on the bed, lying flat on her stomach. She turned away from the TV screen and gave him a coy smile. He smiled back and returned to his keyboard. Once he was sure that she was absorbed in her program, he got up and went to his writing desk. He opened a drawer and pulled out a letter in an envelope and a key ring with old keys, big and heavy. He did not read the letter, but slipped it into his coat pocket along with the keys. He returned to his computer and made a printout of his plan of action.

He headed for the bedroom, where Lauren was sitting on the foot of the bed watching Larry King. Her hair fell loose over her shoulders, and she seemed calm, peaceful.

"Everything's as ready as it will ever be," he said.

Ten

THE NEXT MORNING AS ARTHUR ATE BREAKFAST, HE read the newspaper for the first time in two weeks, while Lauren looked on over his shoulder. From time to time she would stare at him hard, asking him if he was sure that he wanted to go through with the plan. He no longer answered this question. In the middle of the day they went for a walk by the ocean.

They stood by a spot where the waves crashed against the shore.

"Take a good look at all this: angry ocean, indifferent land, towering mountains, trees, light that plays tricks with colors every minute of the day, birds swooping overhead, fish looking for other fish to eat while hoping they won't end up as seagull food themselves. All of this is in harmony—sounds, waves, wind, and sand. And right in the middle of this unbelievable symphony of life, there's you and me and every other human being on earth. But how many of us ever really see the things I've just described? How many realize what a privilege it is to wake and see, feel, touch, hear?

"Not many people are capable of forgetting their worries for the second it takes to marvel at this extravaganza. It seems that the thing that we all seem to be least aware of is our own life. You're aware of it because you're in danger, and that makes you a unique being. You need others because you have no choice. So in answer to the question you keep asking me, unless I take a few risks, all this beauty, all this energy, would become inaccessible to you forever. That's why I'm doing this, because fighting to bring you back into the world gives meaning to my life. How often will I have the chance to do something that *must* be done?"

Lauren did not say a word; after a moment, she lowered her eyes and stared at the sand. They walked side by side back to the car.

At ten-thirty on the dot Paul pulled up to Arthur's driveway, leaving the ambulance idling as he walked up the outside stairs and rang the bell. "All set," he announced when Arthur opened the door.

Arthur handed him a bag. "Put this coat on, and wear these glasses. They're just plain lenses."

"No false beards?"

Arthur ignored the joke. "I'll explain everything on the way," he said impatiently. "We've got to hurry. We have to do this during the shift change at eleven. Lauren, you come with us, we're going to need you."

"Talking to your ghost?" said Paul.

"Enough, Paul! Come on, get moving!"

Lauren sat waiting for them in the front seat.

"Boy, this thing is old," Arthur said as he got in between Paul and Lauren. "What is this, vintage 1971?"

"Well, excuse me," Paul said, annoyed. "I took what I could find, and now you're going to give me a hard time! Maybe we'd get along more easily if you'd just talk to me in your Mussolini voice."

"I was joking. It's perfect."

"Want the flashing lights and siren, Doc?"

"Paul, this is a matter of life and death. Please be serious."

"Can't do it, old pal. Absolutely not. If I seriously believed that my business partner and I were in a stolen ambulance on the way to lifting a body from a hospital, I might wake up, and your little plan would be dead in the water. So I'm doing my best to be as unserious as possible. That way I'll go on thinking this is just a dream, verging on a nightmare. On the bright side, I've always found Sunday evenings very dull; at least this will be memorable."

Lauren laughed.

"You find that funny?"

"Stop talking to yourself!"

"I'm not talking to myself."

"Okay, there's a ghost in the back! But stop having conversations with it. It makes me nervous."

"Not it. Her! She's a woman, and she can hear everything you say."

"I don't know what you've been smoking for the past few weeks, but I'd really like some too."

"Drive!"

"Are you two always like this?" asked Lauren.

"Pretty much."

"What did you say?" asked Paul.

"I wasn't talking to you."

Paul braked abruptly.

"What's the matter?" asked Arthur.

"Stop this! You're going too far, I swear!"

"What am I doing?"

"You know perfectly well," Paul bellowed. "You keep talking to yourself. It's absurd!"

"I'm not talking to myself, Paul, I'm talking to Lauren. You just have to take my word for it."

"Arthur, maybe this all has to stop right here and now. This is complete madness!"

Arthur raised his voice. "For God's sake, I'm asking you to trust me!"

"You have to explain what's really going on," Paul said in a softer voice. "Right now you seem like a madman, and I fear I'm even madder to be getting involved in this craziness!"

"Just drive, Paul, please start driving again! I'll try to explain, but the story hasn't changed for the past few weeks I'm afraid. You have to do the hard part here: you have to try to believe, and understand, even though it defies both."

And as the ambulance wound its way across the city, Arthur explained the unexplainable to his lifelong friend and accomplice. He told him everything—from the beginning, from the bathroom closet to that very night.

Forgetting for a moment that Lauren was there, Arthur added, "She's beautiful, Paul, and she's funny, and witty, and we talk about everything. Oh, we disagree and bicker sometimes, but an amazing tenderness has grown between us. I feel at home with her."

Paul cut in, "If she's really here, you've landed yourself in deep trouble, my friend."

"How so?" Arthur asked, looking at Paul.

"Because," said Paul with a complacent smile, "I think

you just told her you love her." Paul glanced over at his friend, then added, "In any case, *you* believe your story."

"Of course I believe it. But why do you say that?"

"Because I swear you just blushed and I've never seen you blush before." Then Paul called out, "Are you there, young lady whose body we're going to steal? If you are, you can take it from me that my buddy here has it bad. I've never seen him like this before."

Deliberately avoiding eye contact with Lauren, Arthur interjected, "Shut up and drive."

"I'll tell you what. I'm going to believe your story, Arthur. Since you're my friend, I can't do otherwise. Being a friend is all about being willing to act as crazy as the other guy, right? Hey, there's your hospital."

Lauren couldn't remain silent any longer. "You two are pure Abbott and Costello." She was smiling radiantly.

"Where do I go now?" asked Paul.

"Drive to the ambulance bay and park. Turn on the lights."

The three of them got out and walked in to the reception desk, where a clerk greeted them.

"What are you bringing us?"

"Nothing, we are here to pick up a patient," Arthur replied in an authoritative voice.

He presented himself as Dr. Bronswick. He had come to take charge of a patient, Lauren Kline, who was scheduled for transfer to an extended-care facility tonight.

The nurse on duty, a petite blonde named Kate, her name tag said, asked for the transfer forms, and Arthur handed her the sheaf of papers. Her whole being seemed to frown. "Why on earth did you choose to show up just as we're changing shifts? The transfer will take at least half an hour, and I'm due to go off duty in five minutes."

Arthur apologized: he and the driver had had other patients ahead of this one.

"I'm sorry too." Kate told them the patient was on the fifth floor, Room 505, and directed them to the elevators. She would sign the paperwork, leave it on the driver's seat in the ambulance, and notify her replacement. "This was no time of night for a transfer!"

Arthur couldn't resist telling her that it was never a good time for a transfer: it was always too early or too late. Kate ignored his remark.

"I'll get the gurney," said Paul to cut short their exchange. "See you up there, Doctor."

Kate offered to call an orderly to help. Arthur declined, but asked her if she would be kind enough to leave Lauren's medical records in the ambulance with her other papers.

"The records stay here. A copy will be mailed to you, you should know that." Suddenly she looked suspicious.

"I know that, Kate," said Arthur. "I only need her most recent labs—blood sugar, chem screen, CBC, hematocrit, blood gases."

"Wow! That was really impressive," whispered Lauren. "Where did you pick all that up?"

"TV," Arthur joked back in a whisper.

Kate looked at him oddly. "You'll find the lab reports in Miss Kline's chart at the fifth-floor nurses' station." She paused, eyeing him coldly. "I think it's best if I come with you."

Arthur thanked her, but said she should remain here so that she could finish her shift at the appointed time; he would manage without her. "It's Sunday night, and if you're as beat as I am, you've earned your rest." He gave her his most charming, complicitous smile.

Paul, just then returning to the reception area with the gurney, took Arthur by the arm and walked him swiftly down the corridor. The elevator whisked the three conspirators to the fifth floor. As the doors opened, Arthur said to Lauren, "So far, so good."

"Yes!" Lauren and Paul said in unison.

A young medical student burst out of a room, looking frantic. Catching sight of them, he ran over, peered at Arthur's name tag, and grabbed his elbow. "Dr. Bronswick! Thank God you're here. I need help in five oh eight. Follow me!"

The student ran back to the room he had just left.

Arthur started to panic. "This is terrible! How can we get out of this!"

"You're asking me?" said Paul.

"No, I'm asking Lauren!"

"Let's go, you've got no choice," said Lauren. "I'll tell you what to do."

"Yes, let's go, we've got no choice," said Arthur aloud.

"What do you mean, let's go? You're not a doctor, don't you think we should stop this madness before you kill someone?"

"She's going to help us."

"Oh, well, in that case, if *she's* going to help us," said Paul, raising his arms. "Lord, why me? Why me?"

All three of them pushed into Room 508. The medical student stood by the bed, a nurse beside him. He said to Arthur in a panic, "He's gone into cardiac arrhythmia, he's an advanced diabetic, I don't know how to reestablish normal rhythm. I'm only in my third year."

"Never fear, Dr. Bronswick is here," Paul muttered under his breath.

Lauren whispered into Arthur's ear, "Tear off the strip coming out of the EKG machine and hold it up so I can read it too."

"Let's have some light here," Arthur said authoritatively.

He went around the bed and tore off a long strip of the EKG tracing. Unrolling it, he turned his back on the others so Lauren could see the tape.

"It's a ventricular arrhythmia. He's useless!"

Arthur repeated the diagnosis word for word: "It's a ventricular arrhythmia. You're useless!"

Paul rolled his eyes, wiping his hand across his forehead.

"I know it's a ventricular arrhythmia, Doctor," said the student, "but what do we do about it?"

"You don't know anything? What do you mean, *what do we do about it?*" Arthur repeated, stalling for time.

"Ask him what he's already injected," said Lauren.

"What have you injected so far?"

The nurse replied, her tone betraying her exasperation at the medical student's ineptitude, "Nothing! We haven't injected anything, Doctor. We haven't treated the patient at all."

"Tell me what you think we should do," Arthur said, pretending to address the medical student.

"Shit," cried Paul. "We're not here to give medical students lessons. Look at that poor guy in the bed, he's turned blue! You're losing him, buster, I mean Doctor." Paul was beside himself. "San Quentin," he moaned, "next stop San Quentin!"

"Calm down, buddy." Arthur turned to the nurse. "Forgive him, he's new, but he was the only driver available tonight."

"Give him two milligrams of epinephrine, and we'll place a central tract to drain off the fluid. From now it will be tricky, sweetheart," said Lauren.

"Inject two milligrams of epinephrine," Arthur intoned.

"I already have it drawn up, Doctor," said the nurse. "I was waiting for someone who knew what they were doing to give the order."

"Then we'll place a central catheter," said Arthur, his tone half-questioning, half-commanding. "Do you know how to place a central catheter?" he asked the student.

"Ask the nurse to do it, she'll be delighted. Doctors never let them do any of the good stuff," said Lauren.

"I've never done one," said the student.

"Nurse, you can handle this, right?" said Arthur.

"No, you go ahead, Doctor, it'll save time. I'll prepare it for you straightaway. But thanks for your vote of confidence. Come with me," she said to the medical student, like a mother to a recalcitrant child. "At least you can help with the supplies." The nurse left the room with the med student following sheepishly at her heels.

"What do I do now?" asked Arthur, his voice stifled, panic-stricken.

"We're getting out of here, that's what we do," said Paul. "We're out of here and running, right now!"

Lauren interrupted, "You can do this, Arthur. I'll talk you through it."

As she was speaking, the nurse returned with a tray holding a cardiac needle, catheter, and other supplies.

"Stand over him, aim for two fingers below the sternum—you know where the sternum is, don't you? I'll tell you if you're not in the right place. Hold it at a fifteen-degree angle and then push the needle in, slowly but firmly. If you're in the right place, you'll see clear fluid flow back into the syringe. If you miss, it'll be blood. And pray you have beginner's luck—because if you don't, we're in it up to our ears. Us and the guy lying there."

"I can't do this," Arthur muttered under his breath.

"You have no choice, nor does he. This man is going to die if you don't."

"Did you call me sweetheart, or was I dreaming?"

Lauren smiled. "Go ahead, and take a deep breath before you stick the needle in." The nurse handed the tract tube to Arthur. "Take it by the plastic end, and good luck!" Arthur placed the needle where Lauren had told him. The nurse watched attentively. "That's perfect," murmured Lauren, "tilt it down a little more. Now, in one movement." The needle popped through the membrane surrounding the heart. "That's good. Now, turn that little valve on the side of the tube." Arthur did as he was told. An opaque fluid started trickling into the tube.

"Bravo. Done like a pro! You just saved his life!"

Paul had already come close to fainting several times. "I don't believe this," he kept muttering.

The patient's heart, free of the fluid that had been compressing it, resumed a normal beat. The nurse thanked Arthur and said, "I'll take over now." Arthur and Paul made their farewells and went back into the corridor.

But Paul could not resist poking his head back into the room and calling to the student, "Useless." Returning to Arthur he said, "God, you really had me scared there."

"She helped me. She told me what to do every step."

Paul shook his head. "Any minute now I'm going to

wake up, and when I phone to tell you about the nightmare I'm having, you'll laugh. Boy, will you laugh!"

"Come on, Paul, let's do what we came here to do."

They entered Room 505. Arthur pushed the light switch and the fluorescent tubes shimmered into life. Paul went to the bed and looked down at Lauren's body. "You're right, pal, she's a knockout. A little on the pale side, though, almost ghostly, wouldn't you say?"

Arthur laughed. "Okay, pal, enough looking; now wheel the stretcher in beside the bed."

Arthur gently lifted Lauren's body behind her back. "Now, get your hands under her knees, and watch out for the IV. We'll lift her on the count of three. One. Two. Three!"

They gently hoisted Lauren's body onto the gurney. Arthur draped blankets over her, unhooked the IV bag from its pole and looped it over a hook above her head.

"Phase one accomplished. Now let's get back downstairs. No need to hurry, we're just going about our business."

"Yes, Doctor," said Paul, gritting his teeth.

"You guys are doing really well," said Lauren.

As they headed for the elevator, the nurse called to them from the end of the corridor.

Arthur slowly turned around. "Yes, Nurse?"

"Everything's under control here, do you need a hand?"

"No, everything's fine here too."

"Thanks again, Doctor."

"Don't mention it."

The doors opened and they entered the elevator. Arthur and Paul both gave a sigh of relief.

"Three top models, a couple of weeks in Hawaii, a Ferrari, and a yacht."

"What are you talking about?"

"My fee, I'm just beginning to calculate what you owe me for tonight, and that's just for phase one, as you call it."

The hall was deserted when they emerged from the elevator. They crossed it with hurried steps and loaded Lauren's body into the back of the ambulance. On Arthur's seat were the transfer papers and a small yellow Post-it note: *Call me tomorrow, there are a couple of blanks that need filling in on the transfer form. Kate (415) 555-0000, extension 2154.*

Lauren told Arthur she'd ride in back with her body. "It's the first time I've had sole possession of it in months!" she joked. Arthur climbed in next to Paul and they took off.

"So, body snatching is pretty easy after all," said Paul.

"I guess it's because not a lot of people want to do it," said Arthur.

"Yeah. I can understand why. Where to now, Doc?"

"First stop my apartment."

The ambulance climbed back up Market Street and turned onto Van Ness. The neighborhood was quiet.

Arthur's plan called for an initial detour to transfer Lauren's body from the ambulance to his car. While Paul was returning the "borrowed" vehicle to his stepfather's shop, Arthur would bring down everything he had prepared for the drive and their stay in Carmel.

The medical supplies had been carefully wrapped and stored in the front section of his refrigerator.

Reaching the apartment building, Paul tried to activate the garage door, but there was no response.

"This is exactly like a bad B movie," Paul said.

"What's the matter?" asked Arthur.

"In a bad B movie you'd drop the polite manner; you'd deliver a line out of the corner of your mouth. 'What the hell's going on?' is what you'd say. Well, in this case, it's your garage door that's not opening. There's an ambulance stolen from my stepfather's garage parked in front of your driveway with a corpse inside at just the time your neighbors come out to take their dogs for a piss."

"Shit!"

"That about sums it up."

"Hand me that remote."

Paul passed it across with a shrug, and Arthur jabbed frantically at the button. Nothing happened.

"On top of it all, he thinks I'm a moron," Paul groaned.

"It must be the battery."

"All geniuses get stung by this kind of detail sooner or later," said Paul sarcastically.

"Paul, go circle the block while I find a new battery."

"Better pray you've got one in the bottom of a drawer somewhere."

"Don't argue, just go on up," said Lauren.

Arthur left the ambulance and raced up the stairs. He looked in the kitchen, the bathroom, the bedroom. By the time Paul was making his fifth circuit, Arthur had ransacked every drawer in the house and still hadn't found a battery.

"I'm dead meat if the cops decide to pull me over," Paul grumbled. As he began his sixth circuit, a patrol car appeared. "I *am* dead meat!"

The car pulled alongside him; the officer signaled him to lower his window.

"You lost?"

"No, I'm waiting for my partner. He's gone to get some stuff from his apartment, then we're taking Daisy back to the garage."

"Who's Daisy?" asked the policeman.

"This ambulance. It's her last tour of duty, she's done

her time, we've been together for ten years, Daisy and me. It's hard to say good-bye, know what I mean? A whole lot of memories, a big piece of my life."

The cop nodded. He understood and merely asked Paul not to take too long. People would start calling in to report him. Folks in this neighborhood were nosy and prone to worry. "Don't I know it, Officer, I live around here. Good night!" The officer returned the greeting, and the patrol car pulled away. Inside, the driver bet his partner ten dollars that Paul wasn't waiting for anyone.

"I bet he can't bring himself to turn in his old lady. Ten years together, that's a long time."

"Yeah! Funny though. Most EMS guys are always complaining that the city won't give them the money for new equipment."

"Yeah, but ten years, you really get attached."

"That's for sure."

Arthur stood in the middle of the living room, racking his brain for where he might find a battery.

"The TV remote," Lauren said softly.

He spun around to look at her, then grabbed for the little black device. He tore off its tiny rear flap and removed the battery, quickly transferring it to the garage-door remote. Then he ran to the window, leaned out, and pressed the button.

Paul, was beginning his ninth circuit when he saw the door start to rise. He drove right in, praying that the door would close faster than it had opened. "It really was the battery. And I'm in business with him!"

Meanwhile, Arthur hurried down the stairs to the garage.

"Everything okay?"

"For you or for me? Truthfully, I'm ready to strangle you."

"Why don't you help me instead? We still have work to do."

"I've done nothing but help!"

They carried Lauren's body with great care. They sat her in the back of Arthur's car, the IV bag wedged between the armrests, and wrapped her in a blanket. Her head rested against the door. Anyone looking inside would assume she was asleep.

"He really has helped," said Lauren, coming back from upstairs.

"You're right, let's keep things moving."

"I'm right even when I don't say a thing?" Paul grumbled.

"Go to your father's garage and I'll come pick you up in ten minutes. I'm going back up to fetch the equipment."

Paul climbed into the ambulance and left; this time the garage door opened without incident. Crossing Union Street, he failed to notice the same squad car that had stopped him earlier.

"Let a car in between us and follow him," said the policeman.

The ambulance turned into Van Ness, followed at a short distance by city patrol vehicle 627. When Paul drove into the body shop ten minutes later, the police slowed down, then returned to their usual rounds.

A quarter hour later, Arthur appeared. Paul came into the street and got into the passenger seat of the Saab.

"You took the scenic route?"

"I drove slowly, because of her. You can relax now, Paul. We've almost made it. You've just done me an incredible favor. I know you've taken huge risks, and I know it was a lot to ask. What I don't know is how to tell you how grateful I am."

"You want to show me how grateful you are? Just let me drive the Saab. I can't stand thank-yous. Where to?"

"We're going to a place that's also in a deep coma, and the three of us are going to wake it up. We're going to Carmel."

The car left the city on 280 South. Soon they veered off toward Pacifica and then on to Route One, the highway leading along the cliffs to Monterey Bay and Carmel. It was the route that Lauren and her old Triumph had been headed for early one morning the previous summer.

The scenery was spectacular; the cliffs made pale lace patterns against the blackness of the night. A waning moon shed its pale glow on the freeway, which, even at this hour, had its lone travelers and trucks. They drove to the sound of a Samuel Barber concerto for violin.

While Paul drove, Arthur stared out into the night. He knew the enormity of what he was doing. At the end of this journey, another awakening was in store for him. The awakening of the sense of wonder he'd missed for so long, the wonder of Lili . . . and now of Lauren.

Eleven

His mother, Lili, as he called her, was a French poet. She had come to California to marry his father, a pilot, who died when Arthur was three. "His plane flew so high in the sky that it got tangled up in the stars," his mother had told him. She had mourned her husband for a long time, or so it seemed. They stayed in their large white wooden house overlooking the ocean where Lili tended her vast garden. Anthony, an old friend of Lili's, lived in the guesthouse. He was a painter and Lili had "taken him in." He helped her with the house and the upkeep of the grounds, and in the evening he and Lili would talk long into the night. For Arthur, Anthony was a friend and a male presence lacking in his life since his father's death. But Lili was Arthur's best friend. She taught him everything the human heart holds dear. Sometimes she would wake him up early just to show him a beautiful dawn, and to explain how to listen to the cacophony of the breaking day.

She taught him the names of every flower in the garden, how, just from a leaf's design, you could tell the tree whose sap had fed it. She would take him around the garden, showing him the places where she had tamed nature and others where she deliberately let it run wild.

During the green and amber seasons, she would have him recite the names of the birds that interrupted their long flights to seek rest in the heights of the sequoias. In the vegetable garden, lovingly tended by Anthony, she showed him how to harvest the vegetables that seemed to him to have sprung up by magic, "but only pick the ripe and ready ones." At the water's edge, she had him count the waves that on calm days gently lapped against the rocks, as though seeking forgiveness for their violence in other seasons. She taught him to "inhale the breath of the ocean, its pulse, its changing moods. The sea holds our gaze, as the land holds our feet." She explained how to forecast coming shifts in the weather by studying the fluctuations of wind and clouds. She was seldom wrong. Arthur knew every remote inch of their garden; he could have walked it backward with his eyes closed; it held not a single secret. Every burrow in it had a name, just as every animal that chose it for a final resting place had its tomb. But more than anything else, Lili taught him to love to tend the roses. The rose garden was full of magic, a place where a hundred different scents mingled. Lili used to take him there and tell him stories where children dreamed of being grown-ups, and grown-ups dreamed of being children again. Of all the flowers, roses were her favorites.

One summer morning, at first light, she woke him up. "Come on, sweetheart, or the sun will get there first."

The little boy caught his mother's fingers, squeezed them in his small hand, and laid his cheek against her palm.

Lili's hand had a smell that would never fade from Arthur's memory, a blend of different fragrances that she combined herself and dabbed on her neck each morning while sitting at her dressing table.

"I'll wait for you in the kitchen."

Arthur stretched, yawned, and pulled on old cotton pants and a heavy gray pullover. He dressed in silence, for his mother had taught him to respect the stillness of dawn. Knowing exactly where they would be going after breakfast, he tugged on his rubber boots. Then he went down to the big kitchen.

"How are you this morning, my little pumpkin?"

"Fine."

"But you look tired. Were you reading again under your covers with your flashlight?"

"No."

"You know why you and I get on so well? Because I never tell you any lies, because I talk to you just like a grown-up. I trust you. Grown-ups are often scared because they don't know what's important in life. That's what I'm trying to teach you. Think about all the little things going on right now to make this a happy moment. You and me, us talking, the sunrise, the smell of coffee"—she smiled— "and you looking at my hands—avoiding my eyes."

She rose, picked up their bowls, and put them in the enamel sink. Then she sponged off the tabletop and slid the tiny heap of crumbs into the hollow of her outstretched hand. By the door there was a woven straw basket full of fishing lines. Rolled up in a napkin on top were bread, cheese, and salami. Putting the basket over her arm, Lili took Arthur's hand.

Together they negotiated the path down to the small dock.

"Look at all those little boats, all that color."

As always, Arthur waded into the sea, unhitched the rowboat from its metal ring, and hauled it to the shore. Lili set her basket down in it, then climbed aboard.

"Okay, you can start rowing now."

With Arthur straining at the oars, they moved away from the beach. Well before the shoreline was out of sight, he stopped and pulled the oars inboard. Lili had already taken out the fishing lines and baited several hooks. As usual, though, she had fixed only one line for him; for the next, much to his disgust, he would have to thread the small, wriggling, red worm onto the hook with his own fingers. Holding the cork reel steady between his feet on the floorboards, he slipped the nylon thread around his finger and flipped the baited hook over the side, and the little lead weight attached to it swiftly dragged it under. If they were in a good spot, he would soon hook a fish.

They sat face-to-face. Neither had spoken for a few minutes when she suddenly looked straight at him and said in a voice he had never heard before, "Arthur, you know I can't swim. What would you do if I fell in the water?"

"I'd jump in after you," he answered immediately.

Without warning, Lili became angry. "That's plain stupid!" Arthur was stunned by the vehemence of her voice. "What you'd do is try to make it back to the shore. Your life is all that matters. Don't ever forget it. It's a unique gift and you must promise me that you'll never take chances with it. Promise me!"

"I promise."

"No, you wouldn't jump in after me," she said more

gently. "What you'd do would be this: you'd stretch your arm out to see if you could help me back on board. If you couldn't, and I drowned, you would know that you had tried. You would have peace of mind. You'd have made the right decision by deciding not to risk dying for nothing, but you'd have done everything you could to save me."

Arthur began to cry. Lili collected her son's tears on the back of her forefinger.

"Sometimes we are powerless in the face of our impulses; when we feel helpless, we're frightened, and fear dulls our reactions. It makes us weak. You're going to be scared in lots of ways, Arthur. But always fight back, and never substitute hesitation for fear. Think, decide, and then act! Don't have doubts, because the inability to act on our decisions leads to a kind of unhappiness that eats away at the heart. Every decision you make can teach you to know yourself better, to understand yourself.

"Move the world, your world! Look at the landscape around you, see how beautifully sculpted the coast is. See how the sun brings it to life with a thousand different lights and hues. And every tree on the shoreline there, each dancing to the wind to its own sweet time. Do you think nature was afraid to create so many details, so much texture and color? But the most beautiful thing that the earth has given us humans is the thing that *makes* us human—the joy of sharing. Anyone who does not know how to share is only half-alive in his heart.

"You see, Arthur, this early morning that we're spending together will be engraved in your memory. Later, when I'm not here anymore, you'll think back to it and the memory of it will be sweet, because this is a moment we've shared. And if I fell in the water, you wouldn't jump right in to rescue me, that would be dumb."

Lili left as elegantly as she had lived. On the morning she died, the little boy went to his mother's bed.

"Why?"

Anthony, standing beside the bed, said nothing. He opened his eyes and looked at the child.

"Why didn't she even say good-bye to me? I'd never have done anything like that, never. How could she leave me while I was sleeping?"

Sometimes a child looks at you in such a way that you are taken back far in time, in memory, so it is impossible not to answer the child's questions.

Anthony put his hands on the boy's shoulders. "What else could she do? You don't ask death to come calling: it just comes. Your mother woke in the middle of the night in terrible pain. She wanted to wait for the sun to rise, but in spite of her determination to stay awake, she fell gently asleep."

"It's my fault then. I was sleeping."

"No, it isn't, of course it isn't, you mustn't look at it that way. Do you want to know the real reason your mom left without saying good-bye? She was a great lady, and all great ladies know how to leave in dignity, leaving those they love to get on with their lives."

The boy looked straight into the man's sorrowing eyes and sensed an emotion that he had only guessed at so far. His eyes followed the tear rolling down the man's cheek and winding its way through the stubble on his chin. Anthony brushed his eyes with the back of his hand.

"Well, as you can see, I'm crying. Go ahead. You can too."

Arthur fought back his tears almost as if he wanted to stop time.

"Little one, your life lies ahead of you, not in your past. That's what she was trying to teach you. Remember that, Arthur."

"Please leave me alone with her. I thought death would scare me, but she looks beautiful."

He looked at his mother's hand, the blue veins that flowed under the soft skin. He took it to his lips and slowly stroked his cheek with it before kissing her palm.

"I love you. I'll always love you and I'll make you proud of me."

"Arthur?" said Anthony.

"Yes."

"I have a letter for you." Anthony handed Arthur an envelope. "I'll leave you alone now."

Arthur sniffed the heavy, cream-colored paper and inhaled his mother's scent before he unsealed it.

> My dear Arthur,
>
> When you read this letter, I know that deep down you'll be mad at me for playing this dirty trick on you. This is the last letter I will ever write to you, so call it my last testament of love.
>
> My soul has flown away, carried up high by all the happiness you've given me. Life is wonderful, Arthur, but sometimes it's only when you step back from it that you see how truly wonderful it is. So you must remember to embrace it every day.
>
> At times life has us doubting everything, but don't ever think the flowers won't bloom again, my sweetheart. Since the day you were born, I saw that light in your eyes, and I

knew you were not like other boys. I've seen you fall and get
up with your teeth clenched, when any other boy would
have cried and given up. That courage is your strength, but
it could also be your weakness. Remember that you have to
give in order to receive. Strength and courage can be turned
against you if you don't make proper use of them. Men too
get to cry, Arthur, men also feel pain.

From now on I won't be around to guide you. Too early
the time has come for you to become a man.

But over this long journey that lies ahead of you, never
lose your child's soul. Never forget your dreams, because
dreams are what will perfume your existence; dreams will
be the scent that makes you want to get up and discover
each new morning.

My strong, beautiful, dear boy, always trust your in-
stincts, trust your conscience and your feelings. Live your
life to the full. From now on you're responsible for yourself
and for those you will love. Live up to that responsibility;
never lose that look you had in your eyes when we greeted
the dawn together. Don't let angry or disillusioned people
make you cynical. Trust in the magic. The most important
thing I gave you is your sense of wonder. Don't ever lose it.

My sweet young man, I must leave you; hold on tight to
this beautiful earth of ours. I love you, my darling, you were
my everything, but I'm leaving with my mind at rest. I'm so
proud of you.

Your loving mother, Lili

Arthur folded the letter and put it in his pocket. He
kissed his mother's cold forehead. He left the room with a
firm step, as she had always taught him: *A man who leaves
must never look back.*

He headed for the garden through the cool, sweet morning dew and knelt down by the rosebushes. Then and only then did he let his tears run free.

Anthony watched from the porch. "Oh, Lili, you were the only one he let into his world, you left too soon, much too soon," he murmured.

Then Arthur and Anthony sat together on the porch, but neither of them spoke, surrounded by the memories hidden within these walls.

Finally the child fell asleep in Anthony's arms.

Careful not to wake him, Anthony sat motionless for a long time with Arthur's head cradled on his shoulder. When he was sure the boy was sound asleep, he picked him up and returned to the house. Lili had been gone only a few hours, and already the atmosphere was different. An indescribable resonance and certain smells and colors seemed to be drawing back into their shells, preparing to vanish altogether.

Lili had seen to everything before leaving. A few weeks after her death, Anthony closed up most of the large house. He kept only the two ground-floor rooms open, and there he made his home for what remained of his life. One day, he drove Arthur to the station and put him on a train that carried him off to a family-run boarding school. There Arthur grew up alone. Certainly Lili could not have picked a better place for him. But Arthur took with him the memories his mother had left him, memories that now filled every available space in his head. As a small boy, he was always even-tempered, and the teenager who stepped into the small boy's shoes had the same forthright character, to which he added an uncommon flair for observation. The young man never seemed to agonize over anything. One

June evening at the end of his school years, he received a summons from the principal. She told him that his mother—knowing that she was ill—had come to see her a year before her death. They had spent long hours working out all the details of Arthur's education. Lili had given the principal, Mrs. Senard, the keys to the Carmel house where he had grown up and left him some savings, which would finance further studies and help him start out.

Arthur took the keys from the desk where Mrs. Senard had set them down. The ring was a small ball of silver, with a groove down the middle and fastened with a tiny clasp. Arthur pushed back its little lever and the ball opened. In each half was a miniature photo: one of himself when he was seven, the other of Lili. Arthur carefully snapped the ring shut.

The principal rose to signal that the meeting was over. As they walked to her office door, she took him in her arms and hugged him. She slipped an envelope into his hand and closed his fingers over it.

"This is also from her," Mrs. Senard said quietly. "It's for you. She asked me to give it to you when you finished school."

As soon as she opened the door to her office, Arthur was out and walking down the corridor without looking back.

He knew it would be a long time before he would open either the letter or the door to the house in Carmel.

Twelve

THE CAR WAS APPROACHING THE FINAL MINUTES OF THIS
long night's drive. Its headlamps lit up the orange lines of
the bends carved out of rock cliffs, and the long white lines
of the open stretches, flanked on either side by marshland
and empty beach. Lauren was dozing. Paul drove in silence, focused on the road and deep in his own thoughts.
Arthur took advantage of this moment of peace to remove a
letter unobtrusively from his pocket. It was the letter he
had placed there along with the heavy keys from the writing desk in his apartment.

When he opened the envelope, a waft of fragrance escaped, laden with memories. It was a blend of the two per-
fumes his mother used to concoct in a big yellow crystal
flask with a tarnished silver stopper. The smell released his
own memories of her. He removed the letter and carefully
unfolded it.

My darling Arthur,

If you are reading these words, it means you've finally made up your mind to set out for Carmel. How I'd love to know how old you are right now.

You're holding the keys to the house where we spent such wonderful years together. I knew you wouldn't go there right away, that you'd wait until you felt ready to wake the old place up.

Soon you'll be pushing open the front door. I can still hear it creak. Every room you wake will stir memories. You'll open up the shutters one by one, letting in the sunlight that I shall miss so much. And of course you'll go to the rose garden. Perhaps by now they will have run wild.

You should also go to my study. Make yourself comfortable there. In the closet you'll find my small black suitcase. Open it if you wish, if you have the strength. Inside you'll find notebooks full of the pages I wrote to you every day of your childhood.

Your life is before you. You alone are master of it. Be worthy of "all the things I loved about you."

Your mother, Lili.

Discreetly he returned the letter to his pocket.

Arthur gave Paul directions from the passenger seat. It had been more than twenty years since he'd been here, yet nothing had changed; he recognized the smell of the place even in the dead of night. Arthur saw the cypress that stood herald at the turn onto the dirt road, potholed by winter rains and baked by summer suns. As they rounded a bend, Arthur could make out the ornate, green wrought-iron gate that protected the property from the tourists.

"Here we are," said Arthur.

"Got the keys?"

"I'll open the gate and let you through." Arthur got out of the car and inhaled the fresh, cold sea air. "You go on down to the house and wait for me, I'll walk."

"Is she coming with you or staying in the car?"

Arthur leaned in the window. "Lauren," he called gently.

"You go on alone, I think that's best for the moment," she said.

"You just got lucky, she's staying with you," Arthur told Paul with a grin.

The car pulled away, trailing dust. Arthur stood there quietly for a long time, taking in the dark landscape. Broad strips of ocher-colored soil were bordered by umbrella and silver pines that Anthony had planted when Arthur was a boy and now towered above him. The ground was strewn with pine needles, and in the distance he could hear the ocean. The house looked intact, although the surrounding shrubbery was overgrown. He could just make out the peeling blue wooden fence that enclosed the rose garden off to the left of the house.

When he got to the house, he realized that it seemed smaller than he'd remembered. It needed a good paint job, and several of the closed shutters were hanging precariously, but the roof looked solid. Anthony had taken such good care of it.

Paul had parked by the wide front porch and was waiting for Arthur beside the car. "You took your time getting here!"

"More than twenty years!"

"So? What now?" asked Paul.

Arthur told Paul they would first need to put Lauren's body in his mother's study on the ground floor. Arthur slipped the key in the lock and unhesitatingly turned it the wrong way, which was the right way to open it. Some lessons become automatic, even when not repeated for years. The click of the latch prompted instant recognition, as if he had heard it just the day before. He walked into the hallway and opened the first door on the left. Without thinking, he flipped on the light switch, deliberately ignoring his surroundings. There would be time enough to rediscover this place, and to show it to Lauren, but first they needed to deal with her body.

Suddenly Paul craned his head through the door. "How come there's still electricity here?"

"I called the company Friday and asked them to reconnect us. Same for the water in case you're worried. C'mon, Paul, let's move her right away." Arthur led Paul back out of the house to the car.

Lauren stayed with her body as they carried the stretcher up the stairs and wheeled it into Lili's study. They shifted it onto the sofa bed.

Lauren looked at Arthur. "Now make sure the IV's running freely, check my pulse to make sure it's not racing, then leave me alone here for a while. I need to get used to my new surroundings."

Paul unloaded the rest of the supplies, and Arthur helped him arrange them in the kitchen.

When Paul had finished bringing everything in, he said, "Well, buddy, I'd love to stay for your housewarming party with your comatose ghost, but I better hit the road right away if I want to get at least half a day in the office. Think we might find a way to make me a cup of fuel before I take off?"

Arthur opened the kitchen cabinet and took out a small Italian espresso maker and set it on the stove. He found an old, unopened can of Lavazza in the cupboard and measured it into the cup, then filled the top section with coffee.

"A French mother with an Italian coffeemaker?" Paul asked.

"It was her only concession to the Italians." Arthur bent down and turned the tap on the butane tank under the sink. Then he turned the knob on the left of the stove top to turn on the burner itself.

"You think there's still gas in that bottle?" asked Paul.

"Anthony would never have left the house with an empty tank in the kitchen, and I'll bet you there are at least two more full ones in the garage."

Soon Arthur set two cups on the wooden tabletop and poured out the fragrant coffee. "Give it a moment."

"Why?"

"Because you'll burn yourself, and anyway you have to inhale it first. Let the aroma flood your nostrils."

"Cut the crap about the coffee. You're driving me mad. I can't believe it, 'let the aroma flood your nostrils'?"

Paul raised the cup to his lips, then instantly spat his tiny sip of hot coffee back into his cup.

Just then Lauren came and stood behind Arthur and whispered in his ear, "I like this place. I feel good here, it's soothing."

"I'm glad you like it."

"I can't wait to see the grounds."

"I can't wait to show you everything."

"Are you okay there, mate?" Paul interrupted.

"Sorry," Arthur said, "I was talking to Lauren."

"If you find my presence intrusive, just pretend I'm not here," Paul said sarcastically.

With a slightly mischievous look in her eye, Lauren

whispered to Arthur that she longed to be alone with him.

Paul, waiting testily for Arthur to turn his attention from Lauren back to him, broke in, "Do you still need me? Because if not, I'm heading out now. You know your little talks with Ghostie make me feel uncomfortable."

"Why don't you try being more open-minded?"

"You want me to be more open-minded—me, the guy who stole an ambulance to help you lift a body from a hospital one fine Sunday night, the guy who's now drinking Italian coffee hours from home without having slept a wink. You've got a lot of nerve!"

"I'm sorry, Paul. You know that's not what I meant. And I am grateful to you, more grateful than I can ever express. I truly hope someday I'll be able to return the favor."

Arthur was worried that his friend might be too tired to tackle the return drive. But Paul reassured him: thanks to that Italian coffee (he insisted ironically on the term), he was good for at least twenty hours nonstop before the Sandman would come anywhere near him.

"Now, is it all right for me to leave you and the ghost and the corpse all here alone, without a car, in a deserted house in the middle of the night?" Paul asked.

"Actually there should be a vintage Ford station wagon in the garage, an old-fashioned woody."

"When was the last time anyone drove it?"

"I guess it's been a while."

"And you think 'Ford' will start?"

"It'll be okay as soon as I recharge the battery," Arthur said as he walked out to the car with Paul. "Don't worry about me."

"Of course I'll worry about you. If these were normal

circumstances and I was leaving you alone in this house, I'd be terrified about the idea of ghosts. But you, you bring your own!"

"Go on."

Paul started the car and lowered his window. "You're sure you'll be all right?"

"I'll be fine."

"Okay, then I'm off."

"Paul?"

"Yes?"

"I mean it, thanks for everything."

"It was nothing."

"It was a hell of a lot, you took all those risks for me without knowing the whole picture, all out of loyalty and friendship. It was a great hell of a lot, and I know it."

"I know you know. Okay, I'm out of here—before we start getting sentimental. Take good care of yourself and keep me posted at the office."

Arthur promised and watched until the Saab's taillights faded from view.

Lauren came out and stood beside him. "How long has it been since your mother died?"

"A long time."

"And you've never been back here?"

"Never. You're not the only ghost in my life," he said gently.

"It's difficult for you, isn't it, being here?"

"That's not quite the word; let's say it's important to me to be here."

"And you did this for me?"

"I did it because it was time to try."

"To try what?"

"I forgot you had such a stubborn streak." He paused. "To open a little black suitcase."

"What are you talking about?"

"Undiscovered memories."

"You have a lot of them here?"

"This was my mother's home and mine too for a while."

"Did your mother die suddenly?"

"No, she died of cancer; she knew all about it ahead of time. But for me it was very sudden. Come on, I'll show you around."

The two of them went down the front steps, and Arthur led Lauren to the ocean. They sat on the rocks at the water's edge, shaded by a straggling, windblown cypress.

"If you knew how many hours I spent sitting here with her. We often came down to watch the sunset. Lots of people gather on the beaches in the evening just to watch the show. Every night it's different. Because of differences in the temperature of the ocean, the air, and a host of other factors, the color of the sky at sunset never repeats itself."

"Did you live here long?"

"Until I was ten. That's when she died."

"Tonight you'll show me the sunset."

"In this neck of the woods, it's a must," he said with a smile.

Behind them, the house was beginning to reflect the early-morning light. The facade was a little wind-beaten on the seaward-facing side, but overall the house had stood up well over the years. From the outside, no one would have believed it had been sleeping so long.

"The house is in pretty good shape given that it's been empty for so long," said Lauren.

"Anthony was a meticulous, obsessive caretaker; he was a gardener, a repairman, a fisherman, a nanny, and a watchman. He was an unknown painter who turned up here one day and Mom took him in. He lived in the little outbuilding. He was a friend of both my parents, but I believe he was always in love with Mom, even when Dad was still alive. I suspect they ended up as lovers, but much later on." Arthur explained that they just had to look at each other to know what the other was thinking. He believed that during those shared silences, they healed all the disappointments of their lives, that there was a calm between them that was almost disconcerting. They seemed to be two halves of a perfect whole.

"What happened to him?"

Anthony had outlived Lili by fifteen years. He had retreated into the very study where Lauren's body now lay. He spent the last years of his life looking after the house. He died early one winter. On a cool, bright morning he woke feeling weary. As he was oiling the gate hinges, he felt a dull twinge in his chest. He walked among the trees gasping for air, which all of a sudden seemed in short supply. The lower boughs of the old pine where he had spent his spring and summer siestas cushioned him as he toppled helplessly over. Overcome by pain, he crawled to the house and called his neighbors for help. He was taken to the Monterey emergency center, where he died a few days later. At his death, the family attorney contacted Arthur to ask him what should be done with the house.

"The attorney told me that he was amazed when he went to see the house. Anthony left everything in perfect order, as if he had been about to go on a trip the day he had his attack."

"Maybe that's what he had in mind?"

"Anthony, going on a trip? No. Just going to Carmel for the groceries was an expedition. No, I believe he had the dying elephant's instinct: he felt his hour coming, or else maybe he'd just had enough and just gave up."

To explain what he meant, Arthur told Lauren about his mother's answer to a question he had asked her one day about death. He wanted to know if big people were afraid of it. He remembered her reply word for word: "When you've had a really good day, when you've got up early in the morning to go fishing with me, when you've been running around or working in the rose garden with Anthony, by evening you're worn-out, right? And even though you usually hate going to bed, all you want to do is dive into those sheets. On evenings like those, you're not scared to go to sleep.

"Life is a bit like that day. When you've had a rich and full life, when your body is slowing down, the thought of going to sleep forever doesn't scare you the way it used to."

"Mom was already sick when she told me this. I think she knew what she was talking about."

"What did you answer?"

"I grabbed her arm tight and asked her if she was *tired*. She smiled. Anyway, all that is just to explain that I think Anthony had reached some state of wisdom."

"Like the old elephant," Lauren said softly.

As if with one mind, they both rose and crossed back toward the house. Arthur abruptly left the path, went to the blue wooden gate, and opened it slowly.

"Now for the jewel in the crown—Lili's kingdom of roses!"

Lili was crazy about her roses. They were the only subject on which he had ever seen her squabble with Anthony.

"Mom knew every flower personally. If you dared cut just one of them, she would realize at once." The garden had a staggering variety of species. Lili ordered cuttings from catalogs. She took pride in growing varieties from all over the world, especially ones that were not supposed to be suited to the local climate. It became a challenge for her to refute the horticulturists' prevailing wisdom.

Arthur had counted no fewer than 135 different species in the garden. During one torrential downpour, his mother and Anthony had got up in the dead of night, raced to the garage, and hauled out a tarpaulin that was easily thirty feet across and a hundred feet long. Working with feverish haste, Anthony had fastened three sides of the tarpaulin to heavy posts. As for the fourth side, they had held it up at arm's length, one standing on a stepladder, the other perched on a tall tennis umpire's chair. They had spent the night shaking this giant umbrella whenever it became weighed down with rain. The storm had lasted more than three hours. "I'm convinced they would have been less excited if the house had caught fire. Next morning they looked like two human shipwrecks." But they had saved the rose garden.

"There are still dozens of them," Lauren said.

"Oh, but these are wild roses, the ones you see now. Neither sun nor rain worries them."

They spent a good part of the day discovering and rediscovering the house's surroundings. Arthur pointed out a tree with the carvings he had made on its bark, and he showed Lauren where he had broken his collarbone, falling from a pine. The day passed serenely, with Lauren learning all the details of Arthur's childhood. As sunset approached, they returned to the ocean's edge, sat on a boulder, and gazed at the sight people flocked from far and wide to behold.

When night fell, they retreated to the house, and Arthur gave Lauren's body a sponge bath. Then he ate a light supper, and they settled down by the fire he had made in the little living room.

"Well now, what about this little black suitcase?"

"Nothing escapes you, does it?"

"I listen, that's all."

"It's a case that belonged to Mom. She kept all her letters and souvenirs in it. In fact, I believe the case must contain everything that mattered in her life."

"What do you mean, 'I believe'?"

The case was a great mystery, he told her. Opening it was strictly forbidden. "And believe me, I'd never have risked it!"

"Where's it now?"

"In the study next door."

"And you never came back to open it. I can't believe it!"

He had never wanted to rush this moment. He told himself that he would have to be fully grown-up, and ready to understand what he might find inside. Seeing Lauren's skeptical frown, he confessed, "Okay, the fact is I was always scared to open it."

"Scared of what?"

"I don't know, scared it would change my image of her."

"Go and get it!"

Arthur did not move. Lauren insisted: there was no reason to be afraid. If Lili had packed her whole life into a case, it was so that her son might one day know who she was. "The risk of loving is loving faults as much as the strengths—they go together. What are you afraid of—passing judgment on your mother? You don't have the soul of a judge. You can't ignore what's in the suit-case: you'd be breaking her rules. . . . She left it to you so that you could learn all about her, to prolong what life didn't allow her to. So that you could really know her, not just as a child but with the eyes and heart of a man."

For a few seconds, Arthur considered what Lauren had just said. Keeping his eyes on her, he got up, went out to the study, and opened the closet. The little black case sat on the shelf in front of him. Taking a firm grip on its worn handle, he yanked it. Returning to the little living room, he sat down cross-legged next to Lauren. Taking a deep breath, Arthur snapped the locks and the lid sprang open. The case was stuffed with letters, photos, and memorabilia from Arthur's past—a small airplane he'd carved out of rock salt to mark a long-gone Mother's Day, a modeling-clay ashtray, a seashell necklace, even Arthur's silver baby spoon and shoes. On the very top of the case was a folded letter, sta-pled shut, on which Lili had written ARTHUR in big let-ters. He took it and unsealed it.

> *Dearest Arthur,*
> *So, here you are in your house. Time heals all wounds,*
> *though it leaves us with a few scars. In this suitcase, you'll*
> *find all my memories, those I shared with you, those from*
> *my life before you, and those I was unable to tell you about*
> *because you were still a child. You will learn to see your*
> *mother with new eyes. I was your mother and I was also a*
> *woman, with fears, doubts, failures, regrets, and triumphs.*
> *Much of the advice I gave you came from my own mistakes.*
> *And I made a lot of them. Parents are like mountains we*

spend our lives trying to climb. We don't realize that one day we ourselves will be those mountains.

There's nothing more complex than raising a child. You spend your whole life giving him or her what you think is best, yet knowing all the while that you are constantly mistaken. But for most parents it is all out of love, even though sometimes it's impossible not to give way to a little selfishness. We're not saints, after all. On the day I shut this little case I was afraid of disappointing you. I left too soon for you to see me through more mature eyes. I don't know how old you will be when you read this letter. I see you as a handsome young man. God, how I wish I could have spent more years by your side. If you knew how empty I feel, thinking that I will never see you again open your eyes in the morning, never again hear the sound of your voice calling me. The thought hurts me more than the illness that is taking me so far away from you.

What I want to tell you next is that I have always loved Anthony, but I never fully lived this love. Because I was afraid, afraid of your father, afraid of hurting him, afraid of destroying what I had built, afraid of admitting to myself that I had made a mistake. I feared disturbing the established order of things and starting all over again, afraid that it wouldn't work, that it was all just a dream. But not owning up to my love for Anthony was a nightmare. Night and day I thought about him, but I didn't let myself give in. After your father died, the fear continued—fear of betrayal, fear of hurting you. Anthony loved me the way every woman dreams of being loved at least once in her life. And because of my own unspeakable cowardice, I was never able to return his love. I made excuses for my weaknesses, I wallowed in this two-bit melodrama, and all the time I failed to realize that my life was passing me by at top speed. Your *father was a fine man, but to me Anthony was unique. No one looked at me the way he did, no one spoke to me the way he did; nothing could happen to me while I was by his side, and I feared nothing. He understood all my needs, all my desires, and never ceased to fulfill them. His whole life was rooted in harmony, gentleness, the gift of giving, whereas I sought out battles, I made conflict my reason for being. I knew nothing about the gift of receiving. I forced myself to believe that such happiness was impossible, that real life could not possibly be so sweet. One night when you were very young we made love. I became pregnant but did not keep the child. I never told him, yet I'm sure he knew. He guessed everything about me.*

Today, perhaps, because of what's happening to me, all that is for the best. But I also believe that this illness might not have developed if I had been at peace with myself. We lived all those years in the shadow of my lies: I cheated life, and life could not forgive me. You see, you already know a lot more about your mom. I hesitated to tell you all this (I'm still afraid that you might pass judgment on me). But haven't I taught you that the worst lies are the ones we tell ourselves? There are many things I would have liked to share with you, but we didn't have enough time. It was because of me, of my enormous ignorance, that Anthony did not raise you. When I knew I was sick, it was too late to start again. You'll find all sorts of things in this bag of tricks I'm leaving you—photos of you, of Anthony, his letters (don't read them, they belong to me; they're here because I could never bring myself to part with them). You'll be wondering why there are no photos of your father. I tore them up one night in a fit of anger and frustration, anger toward myself, of course . . .

I tried my best, my love. I did the best this woman could do with all her virtues and defects. But I want you to know that you were my whole life, my whole reason for living, the best, most beautiful, most important thing that ever happened to me. I pray that you will experience the unique gift of having a child; it will help you understand many things.

My greatest pride will always be that I was your mom, and always shall be.

I love you.

Lili

He folded the letter and replaced it on top of the case's contents. Lauren saw that he was crying. She moved closer to him and collected his tears on the back of her forefinger. He looked up in surprise, all his pain washed away by the tenderness in her eyes. She let her finger drop to his chin. In turn, he laid his hand on her cheek, then around the nape of her neck, bringing her face close to his. As soon as their lips brushed lightly, she pulled away.

"Why are you doing this for me, Arthur?"

"Because I love you."

He took her by the hand and led her outside the house.

"Where are we going?" she asked.

"To the ocean."

"No. Here, now." She stepped in front of him and unbuttoned his shirt.

"But how did you—? I thought you couldn't—"

"Don't ask questions. I don't know how I did it."

She let his shirt slide down over his shoulders and ran her hands across his back. He felt at a loss—how do you undress a ghost? Lauren smiled, closed her eyes, and was instantly naked.

"I just have to think about a dress to suddenly be wearing it. If you only knew how much fun I've had . . ."

There on the porch, she wrapped herself around him and kissed him.

Lauren's soul was absorbed by his man's body and, in turn, entered into him, lasting the time of an embrace, like the magic of an eclipse.

The suitcase was open.

PART THREE

Thirteen

INSPECTOR PILGER FOUND THE REPORT WAITING ON HIS desk when he arrived at work. A supervisor from Memorial Hospital had called the police headquarters at 8 A.M., just after she had arrived for her shift. A patient in a coma had vanished from the hospital: a clear case of kidnapping.

He had cursed and grumbled at his more than good friend and colleague Nathalie, who dispatched the calls that came to the central switchboard.

"What did I do to deserve this, first thing on a Monday morning?"

"You could've at least shaved, considering it's the beginning of the week," she countered with a broad but guilty smile.

"That's an interesting reply," he said, stroking his two-day growth. It was true, he should have shaved. But he was only two months away from retirement, and he was already practicing letting his grooming fall to pieces. "I hope you like that swivel chair you're sitting in, sweetheart, because you're not going to be promoted out of it for a long, long time."

"You're a pillar of generosity, George, they should build a statue to you!"

"Sure thing. Then I can be the one to decide which pigeons get to shit on me!"

Bad start to the week, on the heels of the bad week that had ended only two days before.

For Pilger, a good week was made up of days when cops were only called out to settle neighborhood disputes or enforce respect for the civil laws. The very existence of criminal law made no sense, since it implied that there were people twisted enough in this city to kill, rape, and steal— or even to kidnap a comatose patient from a hospital. He would have liked to think that after thirty years on the job he had seen everything. But every week seemed to yield some new example of human depravity.

"Nathalie!" he yelled from his office.

"Yes, George?" She replied, her eyes glued to the daily police bulletin. She was indexing in the reference numbers for the night's reports in the margin created for the purpose. Because the boxes were too small and because the head of the Seventeenth Precinct (her superior, as she liked to call him behind his back) was a stickler for detail, she was painstakingly writing in tiny letters careful not to over-shoot the lines.

"I don't suppose you feel like getting some doughnuts?"

"Nope."

"Oh, come on. I'm not going to be here much longer."

"George, the only way I'd get you doughnuts was if you were retiring tonight."

He jumped up from his chair and came to stand behind her. "Now that's hitting below the belt."

"Hey, I thought that's where you liked it."

"Know where I'm going to shove those doughnuts, ducky?"

"I'm a chick. Not a duck."

"You're a ducky, and an ugly one that can't even fly. Strangely, however, you're my kind of duck. Chick. Whatever."

"Go away. This bird is working."

"Oh, c'mon, why don't you put on your grandma's sweater and we'll go downstairs for coffee."

"And who's going to dispatch the calls?"

"Sit tight. Watch this."

He walked over to the young trainee stacking files at the far end of the room, grabbed his arm, and steered him across to his desk, just inside the front door.

"There you go, tiger, you sit on this nice swivel chair with armrests and coasters." George then pointed to Nathalie. "The lady here has just been promoted to a barstool. You can swivel in this, but no more than two turns in the same direction. When the phone makes a noise, you pick it up and say, 'Good morning, police headquarters, Criminal Justice Division.' Then you listen, you note everything down on one of these pads, and you don't leave to take a leak until we get back. And if anyone asks where Nathalie is, tell them she's having female problems and was last seen running for the pharmacy. Think you can handle it?"

"If it lets me out of going for a coffee with you, I'll even scrub the john, Inspector!"

Pilger ignored the remark, grabbed Nathalie's arm, and hustled her down the stairs.

"Well, your grandma must have looked great in that sweater," he said, studying her with a grin. The red sweater Nathalie was wearing had a holiday theme and was obviously hand-knit. But Nathalie was also a well-built woman and the sweater was also at least a size too small for her, and her breasts seemed intent on bursting through it. God, he loved her body, he couldn't deny it. How lucky was he to have found such a jewel working next to him five days a week for the past four years.

"It'll be so boring around here when they put you out to pasture, George!"

On the corner of the building opposite, a fifties-style sign traced the outlines of a martini glass with an olive in it in red neon. Spelling out the name The Finzy Bar in glowing blue letters above the cocktail glass, the neon shed a halo of pastel light on the old pub's windows. Finzy's days of glory were long past. All that remained were yellowed walls and ceilings, time-worn wooden surfaces, aged floorboards hollowed out by thousands of drunken footsteps and the stumblings of one-night lovers. From across the street, the place looked like an Edward Hopper painting. Pilger loved the Finzy Bar, it felt like home to him.

He took Nathalie's arm, led her across the street, pulled two stools up to the ancient wooden bar, and ordered two lattes.

"Was your weekend really that bad, you big ape?"

"Sweetheart, if you only knew how dull my weekends are. I'm bored shitless."

"Was it because I couldn't have brunch with you on Sunday?"

He nodded.

"Well, why didn't you go to a museum or something? Get out of the house."

"First thing that happens when I go to museums is I catch a pickpocket red-handed, and bingo, there I am back at the precinct."

"Go to the movies then."

"I bust some underage kids sneaking into a R-rated flick."

"Then take a walk."

"Now there's an idea, I can go for a walk! That way I won't look like an asshole wandering down the street. 'So, what's up?' 'Nothing, I'm walking.' Yup, great way to spend your weekend. How's it going with your new boyfriend?"

"Nothing special, but he helps pass the time."

"You know what men's *one* weak point is?" George asked.

"No, what are *they*?"

"They get bored too easily, thrown off track. But I can't see how any man could be bored with a girl like you. If I were fifteen years younger, I'd write my name on all your dance cards."

"But you're fifteen years younger than you think, George."

"Do I take that as a come-on?"

"It's a compliment; at least that's something."

After they finished their lattes, Nathalie rose. "Now, I have work to do and you have to get to the hospital. They sounded frantic."

They parted ways, Pilger to his squad car and Nathalie back to her desk.

When he reached Memorial Hospital, George introduced himself to Head Nurse Jarkowizski. She looked him up and down, from his five-o'clock shadow to his not quite balding head to his slightly pudgy but hard-as-a-rock physique.

"It's terrifying," she said. "Nothing like this has ever happened here."

In the same excited tones, she told him that the chairman of the hospital board was extremely upset. She was sure he'd want to see the inspector that afternoon, before reporting back on the case to his administrators early in the evening. "You will get her back for us, won't you, Inspector?"

"Maybe, if you start by telling me everything from the beginning."

Jarkowizski told him the kidnapping had undoubtedly taken place during the shift change. No one had yet been able to contact the nurse who had been on duty, but the night nurse confirmed that the bed was empty when she had made her rounds at approximately 2 A.M. She had assumed that the patient had died and that the room had not yet been reassigned, following the traditional practice of leaving a bed unoccupied for twenty-four hours following a patient's death. Not until Jarkowizski had made her first rounds had she realized that something was awry.

"Did you ever think that maybe she woke from her coma and was fed up with this hotel and went for a walk? Natural enough when you've been in bed so long."

"I appreciate your wit, Inspector, but why don't you share it with her mother? She's with one of our administrators right now, but she'll be here any minute."

"Yes, sure." Pilger stared at his toe caps. "If it's a kidnapping, what would anyone stand to gain?"

"What does that matter?" Jarkowizski answered irritably, as though they were wasting precious time.

"You know," he said, looking at her hard, "strange though it may seem, ninety-nine percent of crimes have a motive. Meaning that, in theory, you don't lift a comatose patient from a hospital on a Sunday night just for a laugh. And incidentally, you're sure she hasn't just been moved to another department?"

"I'm certain of it. The transfer documents are in reception. She was taken away in an ambulance."

"What company?" he asked, taking out his pencil.

"That's what's so odd. There isn't one."

She explained that when she'd come to work that morning, she had not immediately suspected a kidnapping. Informed that Room 505 was free, she had gone straight to the reception desk to complain. She considered it unacceptable for a transfer to be authorized without first informing her. "But these days, you know, respect for your superiors? Anyway, that's not the problem." The receptionist had shown her the documents, and she saw at once that something was wrong. One form was missing, and the blue form was filled out incorrectly. "I wonder how on earth that idiot let this happen," she had said, mostly to herself.

Pilger broke in to ask for the name of the "idiot" in question.

Her name was Kate, and she had been working at reception the previous night. "It's because of her that we're in this mess."

George was already drunk on Jarkowizski's narrative flow. Since she had not been present when the events occurred, he asked her for the names and phone numbers of all staff on duty at the time of the crime and took his leave.

He called Nathalie from his car phone and asked her to request all the people named to drop by the precinct on their way to work.

By the end of the day he had interviewed them all and

knew that late Sunday night a fake doctor wearing a coat stolen from a genuine doctor (a most unpleasant one apparently) had appeared at the hospital with an ambulance driver and fake transfer papers. The two accomplices had then, with the greatest of ease, kidnapped the body of deep-coma patient Lauren Kline. But last-minute testimony from an intern caused Pilger to amend his report. The fake doctor might in fact have been a genuine doctor: apparently, in an unexpected emergency, the intern had appealed to the suspect for help, and he had taken charge of the situation with great skill. According to the nurse who had also been present, the deftness with which the stranger had put in a central line had led her to believe that he was a surgeon, or at the very least that he worked in emergency services. Pilger asked whether an ordinary nurse could have performed the task. He was told that, yes, nurses were trained for that kind of procedure, but the choices the stranger had made, his instructions to the intern, and his dexterity would lead one to believe he was a physician.

Nathalie was getting ready to go home when Pilger returned to the office. "So, what have you got on this?" she asked.

"Something that doesn't jibe. A doctor who kidnapped a woman in a coma from the hospital. A professional job, no way of identifying the ambulance he used, forged documents."

"What do you think?"

"I don't know. Maybe organ trafficking. They lift the body, take it to a secret lab, operate, remove what interests them—liver, kidneys, heart, lungs—and sell it to clinics that're short on cash and scruples."

He asked Nathalie if she could get him a list of all the private clinics with operating facilities, particularly those in financial difficulty.

"Listen, George, it's six o'clock and I'd like to get home. It can wait till tomorrow, can't it? These clinics aren't going to file for Chapter Eleven tonight."

"See how fickle you are? This morning you were all ready to take me to the prom, and now you're turning down a night on the town with me. I need you, Nathalie, give me a hand, will you?"

"God, George, what a manipulator you are. Anyway, in the mornings you don't even have the same voice."

"Maybe, but it's evening right now. Are you going to help me? Take Granny's pullover off and come to Uncle George's rescue."

"Gee. When you put it that way, how can I refuse? Have a good evening, George!"

"Nathalie?"

"Yes, George?"

"You're beautiful!"

"George, my heart's not up for sale."

"I wasn't aiming so high, baby."

"Did you make that up?"

"No!"

"Didn't think so."

"Okay then, go home, I'll manage."

Nathalie walked to the door, then turned. "Sure you'll be okay?"

"Yeah, yeah, go feed your cat."

"I'm allergic to cats."

"So stay and help me."

"Night, George." She ran down the stairs, sliding her hand down the rail.

*   *   *

The one-man night shift got down to work. Pilger returned to his screen and connected to the mainframe. He tapped out the word *clinic* on his keyboard and lit a cigarette as he waited for the search. A few minutes later his printer began to chatter as it spewed out some sixty printed sheets. Pilger grumpily retrieved the pile and took it to his desk. "Well, is that all? And to find out which clinics are feeling the heat, all I have to do is contact a couple of hundred local banks and ask for a list of private clinics seeking bank loans in the last ten months."

He had been talking out loud, and from the gloom of the front door he heard Nathalie's voice asking him, "Why the last ten months?"

"Cop's intuition," he said as he swung around in his chair, a big grin brightening his face. "Why did you come back?"

"Female intuition."

"Well, it's real nice of you."

"All depends on where you take me for dinner. Think you have a lead?"

"I do, but it just looks too easy. What I need you to do is call central police headquarters and ask whether they've received any reports about ambulances missing on Sunday night. You never know, we might get lucky."

Nathalie picked up the phone. The duty cop at the other end of the line carried out a search on his terminal, but told her there had been no such report. Nathalie asked him to broaden his search beyond the city center, but again the screens drew a blank. The duty officer was sorry, but no emergency vehicle had been ticketed or reported missing on Sunday night. She asked him to get back to her if any new information came up, then turned again to Pilger.

"Sorry, nothing."

"In that case let's go for dinner. The banks won't tell us anything at this hour."

They went to Perry's and sat by the window overlooking Union Street.

George listened absentmindedly to Nathalie.

"How long have we known each other, George?"

"Long enough for you to still tolerate me, not long enough for you to be fed up." But Pilger was in no mood for banter, he couldn't stop thinking about the case. "This clinic thing doesn't work. I keep looking for the motive: Where's the jackpot?"

"Maybe the mother has some ideas. When are you seeing her?"

"Tomorrow."

"Or, maybe she's the one, maybe she's had it with going to the hospital every day."

"No, not a mother, much too risky."

"I mean that maybe she wanted to end it all. Having to see your child in that state day after day. Maybe she just wanted to have it be over?"

"Can you imagine a mother dreaming up a scenario like that to kill her own daughter?"

"No, you're right, it's just too twisted."

"Without a motive we'll get nowhere."

"Okay, let's go back to your clinic lead."

"I think that's a dead end too. It doesn't feel right. Stealing a body for its organs is just too high-visibility. They couldn't hope to do it again. Every hospital in the county would be on the alert, and I don't believe the price of one body is worth the risk. How much would I get for a kidney?"

"Two kidneys, and a liver, a heart; I'd think around a hundred and fifty thousand dollars, maybe."

"A lot more expensive than a T-bone!"

"You're disgusting."

"And you see, that route doesn't lead anywhere either. A hundred and fifty grand would be no use to a clinic staring at hard times. This thing isn't about money."

"Maybe it's about availability," Nathalie suggested.

"What do you mean?"

"A person might be allowed to live or die depending on the availability and compatibility of an organ. People were dying because they failed to receive in time the kidney or liver they needed. Anyone with sufficient financial resources could have masterminded the kidnapping of a person in an irreversible coma in order to save one of his children's lives, or his own."

Pilger found her theory credible but complicated. If they followed up on her theory, it would add substantially to the range of suspects—they would no longer necessarily be stalking a professional criminal. Many people might be tempted to do away with someone already acknowledged to be brain-dead, if it meant saving their own life or the life of their child. In that situation, someone might feel he was absolved of any intent to kill, given the ultimate purpose of his act.

"You think we'll have to do the rounds of all the clinics to identify a financially well-off patient who's waiting for an organ donor?" she asked.

"I hope not, because it would be ball-breaking work, and in tricky terrain."

Nathalie's cell phone rang. Apologizing to Pilger, she picked up, listened carefully, scribbled some notes, and thanked her caller several times.

"Who was that?"

"The duty guy at control, the one I called a while ago."

"And?"

The officer had decided to send out a message to all night patrols, to make sure that no one had noted suspicious activity involving an ambulance, whether or not a report had been filed.

"And?"

"Well, it was a good decision, because a patrol did intercept and tail an ambulance that was driving around and around the Green, Webster, Union, and Fillmoore Streets block last night."

"Smells good. What did they say?"

"They stopped the ambulance driver and he told them the ambulance was going into retirement after ten years' faithful service. They figured the driver had gotten attached to his vehicle and was putting off the moment he'd have to turn it in."

"What was the model?"

"A Ford '71."

Pilger made a swift mental calculation. If the Ford heading for the scrap yard last night after ten years' service was really a '71, it must have been kept under plastic wraps for sixteen years before being put to work. The driver had given the officers a line. At last they were onto something.

"It gets better," Nathalie said.

"How?"

"When the driver finally took the ambulance to the garage, they tailed him. They have the address."

"You know, Nathalie, it's a good thing we're not a romantic item."

"Why do you say that now?"

"Because given the trouble this guy just went to in order

to get this information to you, I'd have proof that you're cheating on me."

"You know what, George? You're a real idiot. I suppose you want to go there right away?"

"No. Tomorrow morning'll do. The garage must be closed, and without a warrant there's nothing I can do. And I'd as soon go there without attracting attention. It's not the ambulance I'm after, but the guys who used it. Better to go there as a tourist; that way, we won't send the rabbits scuttling for their burrows."

Pilger paid the check and they headed outside. "Mind if we take a walk?" he asked. The ambulance had been spotted at an intersection close to the restaurant where they had eaten, and George wanted to at least scan the area.

"Know what would really make me happy?" said Nathalie.

"No, but you're about to tell me."

"If you'd come sleep at my place. I don't feel like sleeping alone tonight."

"Do you have a toothbrush?"

"Yes—yours!"

"Come on, let's go, I want to stay with you tonight. It's been a long time."

"It was just last Thursday."

"Like I said."

By the time they switched off the lights an hour and a half later, George told Nathalie he was convinced he would solve the case.

"Then you will," Nathalie assured him. "As we know, when you're convinced of something, you're only wrong fifty percent of the time."

* * *

Tuesday was a productive day. Pilger had a long, rather painful meeting with Mrs. Kline and absolved her of all suspicion once he learned of the decision she and the doctors had come to themselves the previous week. The mother was obviously shattered, and she did not in any way strike him as the sort who could have organized such an operation.

Next, he had tracked down the offending vehicle at the garage. He was surprised when he first entered the establishment, which contained nothing but ambulances in various stages of repair. It was not the kind of place one could "drop by" unnoticed.

Forty mechanics and about a dozen clerical staff worked there. In all, over fifty potential suspects. The owner listened doubtfully to the inspector and wondered what had possessed the perpetrators to return the vehicle instead of getting rid of it. Pilger told him that a theft would have attracted the attention of the police, who would have made the necessary connections. One of the owner's employees was probably involved, Pilger suggested, and was hoping that the "loan" would go unnoticed.

"Now all we have to do is find which of them was the perpetrator."

"None of them," said the owner. "The lock showed no sign of being forced, and no one but me has a key to the night alarm."

Despite the owner's doubts, Pilger questioned the shop foreman about what might have led the "borrowers" to pick this particular make and was told that a 1971 Ford was the only one that could be driven like a regular car. That was one more reason for Pilger to believe that one of the staff was involved.

Asked whether it was possible for someone to take the

key and make a double, the owner replied, "It's conceiv-
able, when we close the main entrance at noon."

So all of them were suspects. Pilger asked the owner for
the employee records. On top of the pile he put the folders
of all the employees who had left in the past two years.
When he returned to his office at around two, Nathalie was
still not back from her lunch break. He buried himself in a
detailed analysis of the fifty-seven brown folders he had put
on his desk. Nathalie arrived around three, sporting a new
hairstyle and bracing herself for sarcastic comments.

"Not a word, George, you'll only say something stupid," she said before she had even put down her purse.

He looked up from his papers and smiled. Before he
could say a thing, she came over to him and laid her finger
on his lips to silence him. "Something's come up that will
grab you much harder than my hairdo, but I'll only tell you
if you promise to hold the comments, okay?"

He mimicked the expression of someone with a gag over
his mouth and grunted a monosyllabic groan in agreement.
Nathalie withdrew her finger.

"The girl's mother phoned. She remembered something
that might be important to your inquiry, and she wants you
to call her. She's at home, waiting to hear from you."

"But I love your hairdo, it really suits you," he protested
as soon as she was finished.

Nathalie smiled and returned to her desk.

Over the phone, Mrs. Kline told Pilger of her strange
conversation with the young man she had met by accident
on the Marina a few days ago—the young man who had
lectured her so earnestly about the sanctity of life.

She repeated every detail of the encounter. How he had
told her he was an architect; he claimed to have met Lauren

in the emergency room after gashing his hand with a paper cutter. How he also claimed to have had lunch with her daughter often since then. Mrs. Kline did not believe he was really a friend of her daughter's. Lauren had never mentioned him, though he said he had known her for two years. That last detail should certainly help his investigation, she added.

"Well, well," murmured the policeman, "you want me to look for an architect who cut his hand two years ago, who claims that your daughter stitched him up, and you believe we should suspect him because he talked to you about euthanasia in a chance meeting?"

"Doesn't it strike you as a credible lead?"

"Not really, but I'll follow up all the same."

"So what do you think?" Nathalie asked when he had hung up the phone.

"I think your hair looked nicer before."

"Okay, okay, so it was a false alarm!"

Pilger returned to his folders, but not one of them yielded the slightest clue. Thoroughly exasperated, he picked up the phone, wedged it between his ear and chin, and dialed the number of the hospital switchboard. The operator picked up at the ninth ring.

"Well, the time it takes you to answer, a person could die!"

"If you want to do that, I can put you through to the morgue directly," the operator shot back.

Pilger identified himself and asked to be put through to administration. There, he asked whether the hospital computers were able to conduct a search through emergency admissions, by profession and type of injury.

"It depends on the time frame you're interested in," the

woman there told him, adding that, in any case, medical confidentiality prohibited her from giving out such information, particularly by phone.

He hung up on her, grabbed his raincoat, and walked to his car. Impatient, he crossed town, his flashing red light attached to the roof, siren howling. Scarcely ten minutes later, he was at Memorial Hospital. He planted himself in front of the administrator's desk.

"You asked me to find a woman in a coma removed from this place on Sunday night, and now you tell me you can't give me information necessary to my investigation. Now, either you cooperate and can the crap about medical confidentiality or I drop the whole business."

"How may I help you?" Head Nurse Jarkowizski appeared from a nearby doorway.

"I need to know if your computers can trace an architect who was apparently injured and treated here by your missing patient."

"What is the time frame?"

"Let's say two years."

"We'll search through admissions for an architect. It will take a few minutes."

"I'll wait."

Jarkowizski returned ten minutes later. No architect had been treated for the injury in question in the past two years.

"You're sure?"

She was quite sure. Filling in the "Profession" box was mandatory for insurance purposes and to maintain the statistics on work-related injuries. Pilger thanked her. Well, that was one dead end followed through on, he thought to himself as he drove, sans lights and whistles, back to the precinct. But the whole business about the architect and his conversation with the mother began to gnaw at him. When a clue bothered him this way, it was capable of monopolizing his full attention, making him forget all his other possible leads. He took his cell phone and called Nathalie.

"Find out if there's an architect living in the area where they spotted the ambulance."

"Union, Fillmoore, and Green?"

"And Webster, but extend the search to cover that whole section of Pacific Heights."

"I'll call you back."

When he got back to the office, Nathalie told him three architect firms and one architect's residence were in the specified area. Only the residence fell within the first perimeters. One of the firms was located on the next street, and the other two streets away. Pilger contacted the three firms to take a tally of the employees. There were twenty-seven in all. At five-thirty in the afternoon he had over eighty suspects. One of those people could be waiting for an organ for himself or someone close to him.

He thought a moment, then turned to Nathalie.

"Do we have any extra trainees hanging around?"

"We never have anyone to spare! If we did, I'd get home at a decent hour and wouldn't have to live like an old maid."

"Don't be so hard on yourself, sweetheart. Why don't you find me one and have him stake out the house belonging to the guy who lives in our area. See if he can't get me a photo when the guy gets home from work."

Next morning, Pilger learned that the trainee had drawn a blank. The man had not come home.

"Bingo," Pilger said to the young student inspector. "By

tonight I want you to know everything about this man: how old is he, is he on drugs, was he in the service, where'd he go to school, where does he work, does he have a girlfriend, a boyfriend, a dog, a cat or a friggin' parrot? You can call the army, the FBI, I don't care, but we have to know everything."

"I happen to have a friggin' parrot, Inspector," the trainee retorted. "But I won't let that stop me."

The inspector spent the rest of the day morosely trying to make collective sense of the leads he was following. He found nothing to cheer him. While the ambulance had been identified by a stroke of fortune, none of the body-shop employee records pointed to a possible suspect. It meant that many hours of interviews awaited him, and that the chances of solving the crime undercover had disappeared. He would have to question all the architects and their employees working in the general area or living on the block the ambulance was circling on the night of the kidnapping.

And one of them would probably be a suspect because he had stroked the victim's mother's dog and stated his opposition to mercy killing—none of which, as Pilger admitted to himself, exactly constituted a kidnapping motive. A real "shit inquiry," as he thoughtfully put it.

That Wednesday morning, the sun rising over Carmel shone through the faintest of mists. Lauren woke early. She left the bedroom to avoid waking Arthur, still raging at her inability even to make breakfast for him. But she was infinitely grateful that he had somehow been able to touch her, to feel her, and even more amazingly, to love her as if she were a woman in full possession of her life. They had experienced together an amazing array of impossible things, things she would never understand, things she decided to stop trying to comprehend. She recalled what Fernstein had told her one day:

"Nothing's impossible. Only our mind's limitations tell us that certain things are beyond our understanding. Often, we have to solve a whole bunch of equations before we can accept new ideas. It's a question of time and of our brain's limitations. Performing a cardiac bypass, getting a three-hundred-and-fifty-ton aircraft to fly, walking on the moon—it all required work, of course, but more than anything else it took imagination."

Everything she was living and experiencing was illogical, beyond explanation, in violation of every scientific truth she had ever absorbed. It simply was. And for the last two days she had been making love with a man and feeling emotions and sensations she had never known, even when she was alive, even when her body and soul were one. What was most important to her, now, was that it continue.

She took herself over to the beach.

Arthur woke shortly after she left. He searched for her throughout the house, then put on a bathrobe and strolled out to the back and spotted her across the road, sitting on "their boulder." His arms were around her before she even realized he was there.

"Quite a sight," he whispered in her ear.

"You know, I was thinking, since we can't plan for the future, we should close the suitcase and live in the present."

"Today, I'll take you to watch the sea lions swimming over by the headland."

"Real sea lions?"

"And seals, and pelicans, and . . ." He cupped her face in his hands and kissed her.

*　*　*

Thursday morning, the trainee, with some ceremony, delivered the file he had compiled.

"What did you come up with?" Pilger asked before the trainee had even opened it.

"Good news and bad news."

In a show of impatience verging on exasperation, Pilger tapped the knot of his necktie a couple of times: "One two, one two. Testing, testing. All systems go, kid, the mike's working, it's all yours!"

The trainee read out his notes. There was nothing unusual about his architect. He could not have been more normal: he did not take drugs, he was highly regarded in his profession, and naturally he had no police record. He had done his studies in California and lived for some time in Europe, before returning to settle in his native city. He belonged to no political party, was a member of no sect, was an activist in no cause. He paid his taxes and his parking tickets and had never been stopped for driving under the influence or over the speed limit. "In other words, a dull dog."

"And what's the good news?"

"He doesn't even have a friggin' parrot."

"Hell's bells, I don't have anything against parrots, cut it out, will you? What else have you got in that report?"

"His last address, his photo—it's kind of old, I got it from the Motor Vehicle Bureau, taken four years ago, his licence comes up for renewal at the end of this year—an article he wrote for *Architectural Digest,* copies of his degrees, and a list of his bank holdings and real estate."

"How did you get your hands on that?"

"I have a pal in the tax bureau. This architect of yours is an orphan; his folks left him a house in Carmel Bay."

"Think he's vacationing there?"

"Yes, he's there now. And in fact that house of his is actually the 'good news' I mentioned."

"What do you mean?"

"Well, there's no phone there, which struck me as odd for such an isolated place. It was disconnected more than five years ago and has never been hooked up since. On the other hand, he had the power and water turned back on just last Friday. In other words, he went back to that house last weekend. Of course, that's no crime."

"But you're right: that last bit of news could ring the jackpot. You've done a great job. With a mind as twisted as yours, you'll make a fine cop."

"Coming from you, I guess I should take that as a compliment."

"You sure can!" called Nathalie.

"Now," Pilger instructed, "take that photo to the old lady—I'll give you the address—and ask her if he's the guy on the Marina who doesn't like euthanasia. If she fingers him, we're onto something good and solid."

The trainee left the precinct and George Pilger buried himself in Arthur's folder. An hour later, the trainee informed him that Mrs. Kline had identified the man in the photo. But the real break came just as Pilger was taking Nathalie out to lunch. It was sitting right under his nose, but he had failed to make the connection. The kidnap victim's former address was the same as the young architect's. Altogether too many clues for Arthur not to be deeply involved.

"Everything's coming together, you should be happy. So why are you pulling that face?" asked Nathalie as she sipped her diet Coke.

"Because I still don't see what he could be after. This guy doesn't have the profile of a nut. You don't go swipe a co-matose body from the hospital just to give your friends a laugh. You have to have a real reason. Besides, according to the folks at the hospital, not just anyone can place a central bridge."

"It's a central *line*. Not a bridge. Was he her boyfriend?"

Mrs. Kline had sworn he was not. She was almost certain they had never met.

"Some connection through the apartment?" asked Nathalie.

Not that either, the inspector said. Arthur had rented the place, and according to the real estate people, he had landed there by pure chance. He was on the point of signing for another apartment on Filbert, but at the last moment a zealous Realtor insisted on showing him this apartment that had just come onto their listing that day.

"So there's no premeditation in the choice of address."

"No, it's a genuine coincidence."

"Then is he really the guy?"

"I can't say that," Pilger answered thoughtfully. Taken separately, none of their findings implicated Arthur. What was disturbing was the way the separate pieces of the puzzle fit together. With that said—and in the absence of a motive—Pilger could do nothing. "You can't charge a guy because for the last few months he's been renting the apartment of a woman who was kidnapped early this week. At least, I'm going to have trouble finding a district attorney who'll go along."

Nathalie suggested that Pilger call him in for questioning, grill him a little.

The old cop cackled, "I can just hear myself: 'Sir, you rent the apartment of a young woman in a coma who was kidnapped on Sunday night. You had the water and electricity turned back on in your weekend house on the Friday preceding the crime. Why?' And he looks right back at me and says he isn't absolutely sure he understands my question. All I can do is tell him candidly that he's my only lead, and that it would make my day if he really had pulled off this kidnapping."

"So take two days off and tail him."

"Without a court order, anything I bring back will be null and void."

"Not if you bring the body back, and it's still alive."

"You believe it's him?"

"I believe in your nose, I believe in our leads, and I believe that when you're wearing that expression, it means you know you have your man but don't yet know how to nail him. George, the most important thing is to find the girl. She may be in a coma, but she's still a hostage. Pay the check and head for Carmel!"

"Whatever you say, boss." Suddenly energized, Pilger rose, kissed Nathalie's forehead, dropped a couple of bills on the table, and hurried out to the street. During the drive to Carmel, Pilger analyzed, again and again, the architect's possible motives. And he planned how he would approach his prey without arousing his suspicions.

Fourteen

LITTLE BY LITTLE, THE HOUSE CAME BACK TO LIFE AGAIN.
Arthur and Lauren went from room to room, opening shutters, stripping dust sheets from the furniture, polishing, and
throwing open closet after closet.

Thursday was overcast, and down at the foot of the garden the ocean hurled itself at the rocks as if they were block-
ing its way. At the end of the day, Lauren settled down on
the veranda and gazed at the drama unfolding below. The
water had turned gray, with seaweed and matted pine needles bobbing on its surface. The sky darkened to purple,
then black. Lauren loved watching nature fly into a rage.

Arthur sat down on the cushions lining the glassed-in
bay window near Lauren and looked over at her.

"You realize that's the ninth time you've changed since
breakfast?"

"I know, it's because of the magazine you bought. I can't
make my mind up, it's all so fantastic!"

"There's not a woman on earth who doesn't fantasize at the chance to shop the way you do!" He eyed her from head to toe. "You may look great in all that, but come here."

Later, tenderly wrapped around each other, bodies and minds at rest, they remained out in the dark, snuggled close, to watch the ocean. At last they fell asleep, lulled by the rhythm of the ebbing tide.

Pilger arrived at nightfall and checked in at the Carmel Valley Inn. The reception clerk gave him the keys to a small room facing the road. He had barely started to unpack when it started to rain. He stared as the drops fell on the charming streets of the tourist village. Although he lived a mere 120 miles away, he had never been here before. As he stood looking out the window, he felt an urge to call Nathalie. He should have brought her with him. He lifted the phone, took a deep breath, then softly replaced it without dialing the number.

He ordered some dinner from room service, settled down to watch a movie, and was overcome by sleep well before ten.

He awoke the next morning with the rising sun. By eight he had located Arthur's house. By nine the sun had mustered enough ardor to scatter the clouds. At eleven, from his roost up on the ridge, through the pair of long-range binoculars he had been given to commemorate his first twenty years of service, George spied Arthur come out the front door and go to the garage.

Arthur stood facing a tarpaulin thick with dust. He raised it and saw the long lines of a 1961 Ford station wagon. Under the covers it looked like a mint-condition collector's item, a woody from the early surfer days. Smiling as he remembered Anthony's fastidiousness, Arthur walked around the car and opened the left rear door. The smell of old leather filled his nostrils. He could almost hear the motor purr. He sat in the passenger seat, rolled down the window, poked his head out, and felt his hair blown back by the wind of memories. He stuck out his arm, bending his elbow, and his hand became an airplane. He tilted it to modify the takeoff, felt it swoop up to the garage roof and nosedive back down again.

When he opened his eyes again, he saw a small note attached to the steering wheel:

> Arthur, if you feel like starting her up, you'll find a battery charger on the shelf to the right. Step on the gas twice before you switch the engine on. That will start the gasoline flowing. Don't be surprised if it starts with just a quarter turn: that's quite normal for a 1961 Ford. For inflating the tires, the pump is in its box under the charger. A big hug. Anthony.

He got out of the car, shut the door, and walked to the utility shelf. Then he saw the rowboat in the corner of the garage. He approached it and stroked it with his fingertips. Beneath its wooden rowing bench was a long-decayed, baited hook, one of his, the green thread wound around the small cork spool with a rusted hook at the end of it. He marveled at Anthony's sentimentality as he located the charger in the opposite corner, opened the old Ford's hood, connected the cables, and began charging the battery. As he left the garage, he rolled the doors back and left them wide open.

* * *

George's eyes never left his suspect. He watched him set up a table under the arbor, sit down to breakfast, then clear the table. When Arthur sank onto the cushions in the shade of the patio, George took a sandwich break. When Arthur returned to the garage, George followed his movements. He heard the sound of the tire pump and then, much more distinctly, the roar of the V-6 engine starting up after a couple of coughs. He watched the car in admiration as it rolled to a stop by the porch. At four-thirty, just as dusk was coming on, he decided to break off his vigil and get back to the village to glean more information about this odd character.

He called Nathalie.

"So," she said, "are you getting somewhere?"

"Nowhere. Nothing abnormal. Well, almost nothing. He's on his own, he busies himself all day long, he cleans up, fixes things, takes lunch and dinner breaks. I've talked to the local merchants. The house belonged to his mother, who died years ago. The caretaker went on living in the house until he died more than five years ago. None of that gets me very far. He has every right to reopen his mother's house whenever he wants to."

"You said 'almost nothing'?" Nathalie prompted.

George admired her. She never missed a trick. "Because he has some strange habits. He talks to himself, he behaves at his meals as though someone were with him. Sometimes he sits looking at the sea with his arm held out straight for ten minutes."

"What else?"

"At one point he looked like he was giving a girl a long, slow kiss—except that he was alone."

"Maybe he was reliving his dreams in his own way?"

"There's a whole lot of 'maybes' about this guy."

"Do you still think he's got something to do with it?"

"I don't know, sweetheart. In any case there's something not right about his behavior."

"Not right?"

"He's unbelievably calm for someone who's guilty."

"So you still believe it's him."

"I'll give myself another day, then I'm coming back. To-morrow I'm going to pay him a little visit."

"Be careful!"

He hung up, his face thoughtful.

That afternoon, after they had cared for Lauren's body to-gether, Arthur sat at the piano and ran his fingertips along the keys. Although it was no longer in tune, he had made a start on *Werther*'s "Clair de lune," avoiding a couple of notes that were now truly discordant. It had been Lili's favorite piece. He talked to Lauren as he played. She was sitting in her fa-vorite position on the window seat, one leg lying along the sill, the other folded beneath her, her back against the wall.

"Arthur, how long do you intend to go on neglecting the rest of your life?" Lauren asked suddenly.

"Do we really have to talk about this right now?"

"I may remain in this condition for years. Do you realize what you're getting into? What about your work, your re-sponsibilities, your world?"

"What do you mean by my world? I don't have a world. Listen, Lauren, we've been here less than a week and I haven't taken a vacation in two years . . . so give me a little time."

"You certainly do have a world. We all do. Loving one another isn't enough for two people to make a success of sharing a life—they have to be compatible, they have to meet one another at the right moment. And that isn't really the case with you and me."

"Have I told you lately that I love you?" he asked timidly.

"You've given me proof of your love. That's much better. I don't believe in chance anymore, you know. There's a reason that you're the only being on the planet who can hear me. And we got along so well from the very start, at least as soon as you accepted my story. And since then I have this feeling that somehow you know all about me . . . and always have." She paused. "What I want to know is why do you offer me the best of yourself, when you get so little from me?"

"Because all of a sudden there you were, you exist, and just one moment with you is the whole world to me. Yesterday is gone, tomorrow doesn't yet exist. It's today that counts, it's the present. . . . And so I have only one option—to do everything I can to stop you from dying, and to keep you with me."

But that was the problem, Lauren said. Ahead of them was the unknown, and she was terrified of what doesn't yet exist.

"Tomorrow's a mystery for everyone, a mystery that should bring us laughter and curiosity, not fear and rejection." He took her head in his hands, kissed her eyelids, and pressed her to him. "We have now, we have this night, and that's everything to me."

Arthur was cleaning out the old Ford's trunk the next morning when he noticed a dust trail on the crest of the ridge. Pilger drove recklessly down the track and stopped his car by the porch.

"Good morning, can I help you?"

"I drove here from Monterey," Pilger said after he'd gotten out of the car and was holding out his hand for Arthur to shake. "The Realtor told me this house was unoccupied, and since I'm looking to buy around here, I thought I'd come over and see it. But apparently it's already been sold, I'm too late."

Arthur replied that the house had not been sold, nor was it for sale; it was his mother's house, and he had just opened it up. The day was drizzly, and Arthur decided this was an opportunity to show Lauren he could still be "normal." He asked Pilger if he would like to come in for a cup of tea. The old cop declined, saying he did not want to be any more of a nuisance, but Arthur insisted and asked him to take a seat on the veranda; he would be back in five minutes. He closed the rear hatch of the station wagon, disappeared into the house, and returned with a tray, two cups, and a teapot.

"It's a beautiful house," said Pilger as he looked around. "There can't be too many more like it around here."

"I don't know. I haven't been back here for years."

"What brought you back all of a sudden?"

"I figured it was time."

"Just like that, no particular reason?"

Arthur was suddenly uneasy. This stranger was asking excessively personal questions, as though he knew something he didn't want to reveal. Arthur felt he was being manipulated. But he failed to make the connection with Lauren, believing that he was dealing with an entrepreneur of some kind who was bent on forging links with a "future victim."

"In any case," Arthur said, "I have no intention of selling it."

"You're right: you don't sell a family home. That would be almost sacrilege."

Arthur was becoming increasingly suspicious, and Pilger, sensing this, decided it was time to beat a retreat. He announced he was going so that Arthur could go back to his business. In any case, he too had to get back to the village "to look for another house." He thanked Arthur warmly for his hospitality, and both men rose. Pilger got into his car, turned the engine on, and drove off with a wave.

Lauren appeared on the porch. "What did he want?"

"To buy this house, or so he said."

"I don't like it."

"Neither do I, but I'm not sure why."

"Do you think he's a cop?"

"No, I think you're being a bit paranoid. I don't see how anyone could have tracked us down. I think he was some kind of business promoter, or a Realtor checking out the territory. Don't worry. Now, I have those errands to run. Are you staying or coming with me?"

"I'm coming."

Twenty minutes after Arthur pulled out in the Ford, Pilger came back down the track on foot. Reaching the house, he checked the front door and found it was locked, then made a tour of the ground-floor windows. None of them was open, but only one set of shutters was closed. Just one room closed—enough for the old cop to draw conclusions. He did not linger on the premises but returned quickly to his car. Picking up his cell phone, he called Nathalie. It was a productive conversation. Pilger told her he still lacked proof and clues, but he knew instinctively that Arthur was guilty. Nathalie had no doubts about Pilger's intelligence when it came to grasping the right lead, but pointed out that without a court order Pilger had no right to lean on the man, particularly in the absence of a credible motive. He was sure that Arthur's motive was the key to resolving the mystery. And it had to be a substantial one for an apparently balanced individual, in no particular financial need, to take such a big risk. But Pilger could not yet see his way to a solution. He had considered all the traditional reasons, and none of them held water. Now he decided to bluff. He would bombard Arthur with false assertions on the off chance of getting at the truth, blindsiding his adversary and surprising him into a reaction or words that would either confirm or invalidate Pilger's suspicions. He started the car, drove onto the property, and parked in front of the porch.

Arthur returned an hour later and, as he stepped from the Ford, stared hard at Pilger. The cop came over to meet him.

"I have two things to tell you," said Arthur. "First, the house is not and will not be for sale. And second, this is private property."

"I know, and I couldn't care less if it's for sale or not. Time I introduced myself." Pilger pulled out his badge and thrust it in Arthur's face as he said, "I need to talk to you."

"I believe that's what you're doing."

"May I come in?"

"No, not without a warrant."

"You're making a mistake, playing it this way."

"You made the mistake, lying to me. I welcomed you and gave you a drink."

"Can we at least sit on the porch?"

"We can. Go ahead."

The two of them sat on the swing seat. Lauren, standing by the steps, was terrified. Arthur reassured her with a wink, to let her know he was in command and she had no need to worry.

"Tell me what your motive is, that's where I'm stuck." Pilger launched right into his suspicions.

"My motive for what?"

"I'm going to be very frank with you. I know it's you."

"At the risk of seeming a little bit simple, yes, it's true, it's me. I've been me ever since I was born, never any problems with schizophrenia. What on earth are you talking about?"

He was talking, Pilger said, about Lauren Kline. He accused Arthur of stealing her, with the help of an accomplice and an old ambulance, from San Francisco Memorial Hospital last Sunday night. Pilger told him he had tracked the ambulance to a repair shop. He claimed he was convinced that the body was here in this house, and more precisely in the only room whose shutters were closed. "What I don't understand is why. That's what's bugging me. You know, I've been doing this for over thirty years, I'm only a few months from retirement, and believe me, I do not want to end my career on an unsolved case. Frankly I don't give a damn about putting you behind bars. I've done that all my life, slinging folks into the can so they can come out again a few years later and start over. The most you'd get for this job is five years, so I don't care, but I do want to understand why."

Arthur pretended not to grasp a word of what the policeman was saying. "What's all this about a body and an ambulance?"

"I'm going to waste as little of your time as possible. Would you agree to let me see that room with the closed shutters without a search warrant?"

"No!"

"Why not, if you have nothing to hide?"

"Because that room, as you call it, was my mother's, and ever since her death it's been locked. It's sacred to me, like a shrine, it's just as she left it. That's why the shutters are closed. It's been shut up for more than twenty years, and

I'm only going to cross the threshold when I'm alone and when I'm ready. I'm certainly not going to do it for some crazy cop who thinks I'm a criminal." Arthur rose. "I hope I've made myself clear."

"Fair enough. Guess I'll be running along, then."

"Yes, please do."

Pilger rose and walked to his car. As he opened the door, he turned and looked Arthur straight in the eye, hesitated a moment, then decided to see his bluff through.

"If you want to visit that place in the strictest privacy, which I understand, you'd better do it tonight. Because I don't give up. I'll be back tomorrow with a warrant, and it'll be too late then for you to do it alone. Of course, you can decide to move the body during the night, but I'm better at the cat-and-mouse stuff than you. Like I said, I've been at it thirty years, and you'd be opening the door to a nightmare. I'm leaving my card and cell-phone number on the rail here, just in case you have something to tell me."

"You'll never get a warrant!"

"You do your thing, I'll do mine. See you."

With a squeal of brakes, Pilger sped away.

Arthur stood rooted to the spot for several minutes, his heart beating a tattoo of terror.

Fifteen

"YOU HAVE TO TELL HIM THE TRUTH AND TRY TO CUT A deal with him!" Lauren said.

"We have to hurry and find a new place to hide your body."

"No, you can't! He'll be lurking around here somewhere, watching us, and he'll catch you in the act. Stop it, Arthur, this is your life! You heard him, you're risking five years in prison."

But Arthur had a hunch that the cop was bluffing. Without evidence, he would never get a warrant.

"You still have a chance of wriggling out of this. If you save him time in his inquiry, if you give him the answer to his question, maybe he will offer you some kind of plea bargain. Do it now, or it will be too late," she begged.

"It's *your* life that's at stake."

"Arthur, be reasonable, you're just postponing the inevitable. Darling, you have to accept this. You said so this morning, that you believed all this has happened for a reason. You have no choice. You have to tell him the truth."

Arthur turned his back on her and went back to unloading the trunk of the station wagon. For the rest of the day, the atmosphere between them remained tense. They scarcely spoke or even looked at one another.

Later that afternoon she came to stand in his path and put her arms around him.

He gazed at her tenderly. "I can't let them take you, you understand that, don't you?"

She understood, she said, but she could never agree to let him put himself at more risk. "Arthur, we're still together now. I'm still right here. You keep telling me not to think of tomorrow, so let's enjoy this moment, which is still truly ours."

"But I can't experience the moment without thinking of the one to come."

Lauren decided they should play a game. "It's a great game, and it will take your mind off all this. Now, imagine that you've won a contest, and your prize is that every morning a bank will open an account in your name containing eighty-six thousand four hundred dollars. And there are only two rules you must follow: The first rule is that everything you fail to spend is taken from you that night. You can't cheat, you can't switch the unspent money to another account: you can only spend it. But when you wake next morning, and every morning after that, the bank opens a new account for you, always eighty-six thousand four hundred dollars, for the day. Rule number two: the bank can break off the game without warning. It can tell you at any time that it's over, that it's closing the account and there won't be another one. Now, what would you do?"

Arthur was not sure he understood.

"It's very simple: every morning when you wake up, they give you eighty-six thousand four hundred dollars, on the sole condition that you spend it in one day. If you don't spend it all by the time you go to bed, you lose the unused balance. But this game—this windfall—can stop at any moment, understand? So my question is, what would you do if you were handed this prize?"

He didn't have to think long to answer. He would spend every dollar on pleasure and on gifts for the people he loved. He'd find a way to use up every cent offered by this "magic bank account" to bring happiness into his life and the lives of everyone around him. "And even the lives of people I don't know, because I don't think I'd manage to spend so much money just on me and my loved ones in a single day. But what does this game prove?"

She answered, "We all have that magic bank account: it's time. A big account, filled with fleeting seconds. Every morning when we wake up, our account for the day is credited with eighty-six thousand four hundred seconds, and when we go to sleep every night, there's no carryover into the next day. What hasn't been lived during the day is lost; yesterday has vanished. Every morning the magic begins again, with a new line of credit of eighty-six thousand four hundred seconds. And don't forget: we're still playing by that rule. The bank can close our account at any time and without any warning. At any moment, life can end. So what do we do with our daily ration of eighty-six thousand four hundred seconds? Sit here and argue and worry? I beg you, Arthur, let's make the most of all the seconds that we have left."

Since her accident, she told him, she had realized afresh each day how few people understand and appreciate the importance of time. "If you want to understand what a year of life means, ask a student who just flunked his end-of-the-year exams. Or a month of life: speak to a mother who has just given birth to a premature baby and is waiting for him to be taken out of the incubator before she can hold him safe and sound in her arms. Or a week: interview a man who works in a factory or a mine to feed his family. Or a day: ask two people madly in love who are waiting for their next rendezvous. Or an hour: talk to a claustrophobia sufferer stuck in a broken-down elevator. Or a second: look at the expression on the face of a man who has just escaped from a car wreck. Or one-thousandth of a second: ask the athlete who just won the silver medal at the Olympic Games, and not the gold he trained for all his life. Life is magic, Arthur, and I know what I'm saying because since my accident I appreciate the value of every instant. So I beg you, let's make the most of all the seconds that we have left."

Arthur put his arms around her and said softly into her ear, "Each second with you is worth more than any other second."

They spent the rest of the afternoon in each other's arms before the fire. At around 6 P.M., they were interrupted by the doorbell. It was Pilger again: he wanted to apologize for his behavior. Arthur hesitated, not knowing if the man was still trying to manipulate him or if he was sincere. On the spur of the moment, he invited him to come in and have dinner with him. Perhaps he was hoping it would make him seem stronger and more composed than Pilger. Lauren watched as Pilger entered, but Arthur didn't see her melancholy smile.

Arthur set two places and served Pilger a Caesar salad with strips of grilled chicken and even opened a good bottle of Napa Valley cabernet.

"This is so nice of you. I didn't expect you to go to all this trouble."

"What causes me trouble, Inspector, is that you're bothering the hell out of me with your ridiculous theories."

"If they're as ridiculous as you claim, I won't be bothering you much longer. So, you're an architect?"

"You know I am."

"What kind of architecture?"

"My real love is restoring historic buildings and interiors."

"Which means?"

"Giving new life to old houses, trying to find the perfect match between a client's personality and a style of decoration and furnishing. I love to restore a place to its former glory but adapt it to modern life."

Pilger lured his suspect onto a topic that enthralled him. What Pilger soon discovered, somewhat to his surprise, was that Arthur's genuine passion for his work was contagious. The old inspector fell into his own trap: having set out to arouse Arthur's interest and forge some basis of communication, he found his own interest aroused.

Arthur gave him a crash course on the history of San Francisco's architecture, with a glimpse of modern and contemporary developments thrown in. The old cop was mesmerized; he asked question after question and Arthur answered them all. Their conversation went on for more than an hour. Pilger learned how his own city was rebuilt after the great fire; he heard the history of the buildings he saw every day; he listened to anecdotes that illustrated how the houses we live in are shaped by the demands of the geology and climate.

As the cups of coffee followed one after the other, Lauren

listened, stunned by the unexpected kinship springing up between Arthur and the inspector.

As Arthur finished a story about the construction of the Golden Gate Bridge, Pilger interrupted him. Putting his hand on Arthur's, he said, "Arthur, I need to talk to you man to man, and not in my professional capacity." Pilger put his badge on the table and took a deep breath. "As I told you, I've done this for many years, and my instinct has never let me down. I'm absolutely certain that Lauren Kline's body is right now hidden in the shuttered room at the end of that hall. What I still don't understand is why. What's your motive for kidnapping a comatose body from the hospital?" He looked at Arthur, but Arthur remained silent. "You know, you seem like a great guy. You're kind, good-looking, you're well educated, interesting, passionate about your work. You've got everything going for you. So why would you do such a crazy thing as steal the body of a woman in a coma? I just don't get it."

Arthur stood up. "It's too bad. I thought we were really becoming friends."

"We are, that's the point! That has nothing to do with it—or maybe it has everything to do with it. I'm sure you have genuinely good reasons for what you did, and I'm offering to help you.

"I'll be completely honest with you. For starters, I can't get a warrant today: I don't have sufficient evidence. I'll have to go see the judge in San Francisco, negotiate with him, convince him, but rest assured I'll get it. It might take two or three days, enough time for you to move the body. And I guarantee that if you do that, you're going to ruin your life." Pilger paused. "Right now, there's still time for me to help you, and I'm willing to do that, provided you talk to me and explain to me why."

Arthur's reply was tinged with sarcasm. "I appreciate your kindness and your generous offer, and I'm really quite surprised that you feel you know me so well after just spending a few hours with me. However, I too fail to understand something. I don't understand you. Here you are, a guest in my home, I've welcomed you in, made you a meal, yet you stubbornly persist in accusing me—without any proof—of an utterly absurd crime."

"You're the one who's stubborn."

"Why do you want to help me if you think I'm guilty? Just to get another case solved?"

The old cop's reply was sincere. In his career, he had known plenty of cases, crimes of all types, with hundreds of motives, ranging from sordid to silly. But there had always been a common thread between the perpetrators—they were criminals, nuts, maniacs, troublemakers. With Arthur, that did not seem to be the case. So if now, after spending his whole life putting bad guys behind bars, Pilger could help a decent man avoid that fate, "I'd at least have the feeling that for once I was working on the right side of the tracks."

"That's very nice of you, and I mean that. I enjoyed our conversation, but the situation you describe doesn't apply to me. I'm not throwing you out, but I have work to do. Perhaps we'll get a chance to talk again."

Pilger acquiesced with a mournful nod. He got up and retrieved his raincoat. Lauren followed them down the hall leading to the front door.

Outside Lili's room, Pilger stopped, his eyes on the door handle.

"Sometimes it's hard to go back into the past, it takes a lot of strength, a lot of courage."

"Yes, I know, that's just what I'm trying to work up."

"I know I'm not mistaken about you, Arthur. My instinct has never failed me."

Arthur was on the point of asking Pilger to leave when the door handle of his mother's room began to turn, as though someone were moving it from the inside. Then the door opened. Arthur was stupefied. Lauren stood in the doorway, smiling sadly.

"Why did you do that?" he murmured, his voice choked.

"Because I love you."

From where he stood, Pilger at once saw the body on the bed, the IV tubing suspended above. "Thank God, she's alive." He walked over to the bed and knelt beside it.

Lauren put her arms around Arthur and kissed him tenderly on the cheek.

"I couldn't let you ruin the rest of your life for me. I want you to live free, I want you to be happy."

"You are my happiness."

She put a finger on his lips. "No, not like this, not under these circumstances."

"Who are you talking to?" asked the inspector.

"To her."

"Well then, now you really must put me in the picture if you want me to help you."

Arthur looked despairingly at Lauren.

"You have to tell him the whole truth," she urged. "He may believe you and he may not, but tell him the truth."

Arthur turned to Pilger. "Come on, let's go to the living room. I'm going to tell you everything."

The two men sat on the big couch and Arthur told the

whole story. He began with that first evening, when an unknown woman hiding in his bathroom closet said to him,
*What I have to tell you is not easy to understand, impossible to ac-
cept. But if you will listen to my story—if you are willing to trust
me—then maybe in the end you'll believe me. And it's very important that you, in particular, should believe me. For without
knowing it, you are the only person in the world I can share my secret with.*

Pilger heard him through to the end without interrupt-
ing. When he finished his story, Arthur looked challeng-
ingly at his companion.

"You see, Inspector, a story like this just adds another
nutcase to your collection!"

"Is she here, is she nearby?"

"She's sitting in the chair across from you, and she's
looking at you."

Pilger rubbed the bristles on his chin and nodded. "Of
course. Of course."

"What are you going to do now?" asked Arthur.

Pilger didn't speak for a while, then he sighed and softly
said, "I'm going to believe you." He paused a moment to
let Arthur take that in. "And if you want to know why, the
answer is simple. Because to make up such a story and take
the risks you've taken, you would have had to have lost
your mind completely. And the man who talked to me
about the history of the city I have served for thirty years
was definitely not demented. Your story has to be incredibly true for you, otherwise you couldn't have done what
you did. I don't believe in God much, but I do believe in
the human spirit. Anyway, I'm about to retire—and I want
more than anything to believe you, crazy though it seems."

"So what are you going to do?"

"Can I take her back to the hospital in my car without causing her any harm?"

"Yes, if you're careful," said Arthur, his voice full of distress.

"In that case, I'll keep my end of the bargain: I'll get you out of this mess."

"But I don't want to be separated from her, I don't want them to let her die!"

"That's a whole different battle, my friend. I can't do everything." Pilger said he was already taking a big risk by returning the body. And he had exactly the rest of this night and a more than 100 mile drive to come up with a good reason for finding the victim without having any leads on her kidnapper. Since she was alive and had suffered no harm, he believed he could arrange to have Lauren's case classified as solved. There was nothing much else he could do, "but that's already a lot, wouldn't you say?"

"Yes, that's a lot," said Arthur. "Thank you."

"I'm going to leave you two alone for the night. I'll be back tomorrow around eight. Make sure she's ready to be moved."

"Why are you doing this?"

"I already told you, because I like you and respect you. I'll never know if your story is true or if you dreamed it. In any case, from your perspective, you acted in her best interests. A man might almost be persuaded that you were protecting her. Some might go so far as to call it rendering assistance to a person in danger. I don't give a shit. People who possess true courage do the thing that's right. They act when the time comes without considering the consequences." Pilger rose. "Well, enough talk."

Arthur followed him into the dark night. A light mist welcomed them as they went out.

"See you tomorrow," Pilger said, and drove off.

Arthur could not sleep and at first light he went to Lili's study. He got Lauren's body ready for the journey, then went up to his bedroom to pack his things. He walked through the house, closed all the shutters, turned off the gas and electricity. "We'll follow Pilger back to the city," he told Lauren. "We'll go back to our apartment. I know you can't be away from your body for more than a few hours without feeling tired. We'll just have to go on as we were before and hope this has convinced your mother to keep you alive."

The inspector arrived at the appointed hour. Within fifteen minutes, Lauren's body was wrapped in blankets and propped in the backseat of the policeman's car. Soon, the two vehicles were heading back to the city.

Sixteen

Pilger kept his promise. He deposited his inert passenger in the emergency room of San Francisco Memorial Hospital at 11:17 that morning. Less than an hour later, Lauren's body was back in Room 505. The inspector returned to the precinct and went straight to his chief's office and spent over two hours talking there. Nobody ever learned what was said between the two men. But when Pilger returned to his office, he went straight to Nathalie's desk and dropped a fat folder on it. Looking her straight in the eye, he told her to stamp it CASE CLOSED and file it away. When she looked at him questioningly, he added gruffly, "And please don't ask me how, because I won't be able to tell you without you thinking I should have retired last week."

He then went back to the hospital, to talk to Lauren's mother.

*   *   *

Arthur and Lauren returned to the Green Street apartment. They spent the afternoon on the Marina, walking by the ocean. After everything that had happened, they hoped that Lauren's mother might have reversed her earlier decision. They ate dinner at Prego and returned home around 10 P.M. to watch a movie on television.

Their life together seemed to assume a normal course, so much so that with each passing day they were increasingly able to forget their predicament.

In the mornings, Arthur dropped in at his office to sign papers. He and Lauren would spend the rest of the day together, going to movies, taking long walks along the pathways of Golden Gate Park. They spent one weekend at Tiburon, in the house of a friend who lent it to Arthur. Another day they enjoyed sailing and hopping from creek to creek in the Bay.

They went to performances in the city—music hall, ballet, concerts, theater. Time passed by the way it does during a lazy vacation, and they pandered to their every whim. They lived in the moment, without projecting, drawing a veil over tomorrow. They thought of nothing except what was happening in the present. Remembering Lauren's game, they called their philosophy "seconds theory." Strangers passing by assumed that Arthur was crazy when they saw him walking with one arm outstretched or talking to himself. The waiters in the restaurants they frequented were accustomed to this man who sat alone at the table who suddenly leaned over and mimed taking a hand and kissing it, or talked softly to someone who was invisible to everyone else present, or stood back at a doorway to let a nonexistent companion pass through. Some thought he had lost his mind, others that he was a widower living in the shadow of his deceased wife. Arthur had stopped noticing; he was relishing every instant that was weaving the fabric of their love. They were now lovers, friends, companions for life. His partner, Paul, was no longer worried. He managed to rationalize his friend's behavior during the crisis. Relieved that the kidnapping had had no repercussions, Paul focused on managing their office, convinced that his friend would one day return to his senses, and life would resume its routine pattern.

The couple's idyll continued undisturbed for a few weeks. One Thursday night, they had gone to bed after a tranquil evening at home. After making love, they shared the last lines of a novel they were reading together because Arthur had to turn the pages for Lauren. They fell asleep late in one another's arms.

At about six the next morning, Lauren suddenly sat up in bed and called Arthur's name. He woke with a start. Lauren was sitting cross-legged on the bed, her skin pale, almost transparent.

"What's wrong?"

"Hold me, Arthur, quickly. Don't let me go!"

He did as she asked and wrapped his arms around her. Arthur felt Lauren's body becoming less solid in his arms. It was is if she were gradually vaporizing before him.

"Lauren"—he looked at her face, alarmed—"do you feel anything?"

"Keep holding me, Arthur." He held her as closely as he could, pressed the length of her body to his. He was shaking with terror. Her eyes were wide with fear as she said, "It's time, my love, I'm fading away. I'm disappearing."

"No!" He tightened his arms around her.

"God, I don't want to leave you. I wanted this life with you never to end, even before it began."

"You can't leave, you mustn't. Fight it, Lauren, you can't go!"

"Don't say anything, just listen. I have very little time. You gave me what I didn't know existed. I never imagined that love could bring so many simple things. I want you always to remember how much I love you. I don't know what shore I'm going to, but if an afterlife exists, I'll be loving you there with all the strength and all the joy you've filled my life with."

As she was speaking, she became more and more transparent. Her skin became clear as water. Even as he held her, he felt his arms begin to close on a void that was gradually gaining. It seemed to him that she was becoming evanescent.

"Live when I'm gone, Arthur, live every second."

"Don't leave, I beg you. Fight back."

"I can't, it's stronger than I am. I'm not in pain, you know, I just have the impression that you're getting farther and farther away. Your words are muffled, I can't see you properly anymore. I'm so scared, Arthur. I'm so scared without you. Hold me tighter."

"I'm holding you, can't you feel me?"

"Not really, Arthur my angel."

They began to weep together, softly, quietly. Now more than ever, they realized the meaning of one second of life, the value of a single moment, the importance of a single word. They embraced. During a kiss they never finished, she vanished altogether.

Arthur's arms had closed in on themselves. He curled up

in pain. His weeping intensified to loud sobs and cries of anguish.

His whole body trembled; his head rocked uncontrollably from side to side. His fists were clenched so tight that his nails drew blood from his palms.

The "No!" that he continued to howl like a wounded animal resonated in the room, making the windowpanes shake. He tried to get up but swayed and fell to the ground, his arms still wrapped around his torso. He dragged himself to the window seat, where she had so loved to sit, and sat there, numb and devastated. He sat there all day and barely noticed when the sun set over the Bay.

Arthur plunged into a world of absence that echoed eerily inside his head. The vacancy penetrated into his veins and infiltrated his heart. His grief filled him with rage, doubt, and jealousy, not directed against other people, but because of the lost moments, the time with Lauren that had been stolen from him. He keenly felt the lack of the other, of the love he mourned with every fiber of his being, of the body that his flesh still hungered for. His nose sought out a familiar scent. His hand searched for the belly to caress. Through his tears his eyes could no longer see anything but memories. He missed skin seeking skin, he missed the other hand, the one that slowly closed around each finger curling to its own rhythm; he missed the foot that dangled when she was sitting on the window seat.

For long days and equally long nights he remained like this. He drifted from his architect's desk, where he would write letters to Lauren, back to his bed, where he would gaze at the ceiling blankly. His telephone had been off the hook and lying on its side for a long time, but Arthur ignored it. He didn't care, he no longer expected any calls. Nothing was important anymore.

At the end of one stifling day he emerged for air. It was drizzling. Donning a raincoat, he had just enough strength to cross the street and stand on the opposite sidewalk.

The little street—so narrow it suggested a long corridor—was all in black and white. There was only one ray of light on this moonless evening, the light from his own living room window. It stopped raining, but he was still wet. Behind the windowpanes he still sensed Lauren's presence, her graceful movements.

In the shadows of the pavement he thought he could see her supple form disappear around the corner. He thrust his hands into his raincoat pockets, hunched his shoulders, and began to walk.

Along the gray and white walls he followed in Lauren's footsteps, slowly enough not to risk overtaking her. At the mouth of an alleyway, he hesitated a moment, then ducked in, but realized no one was there. Growing numb with cold, he sat down on the curb and relived every moment of a life that had ended too soon, too abruptly.

As a sky that was turning pale announced the dawn of a day without color, Arthur hauled himself to his feet, took one last look, and turned away with the guilty sense of having failed. He headed home.

On the Monday after Lauren had left, Arthur was lying on the living room rug, in the place she had so often lay during their talks, when someone hammered at the door. He did not get up.

"Arthur, are you there? I know you're inside! Open the

door for God's sake! Open it!" Paul yelled. "Open up or I'll break it down."

The door shuddered under the impact of Paul's shoulder.

"Shit! That hurt like hell! I think I've broken my collar-bone. Open the goddamn door!"

Arthur got up and went to the door, flipped the lock, and returned to collapse on the couch. When Paul came in, he was amazed at the devastation. Dozens of scraps of paper were strewn across the floor, all covered with handwritten notes scribbled by his friend. Half-empty food cans littered the kitchen counters. The sink was overflowing with dirty dishes.

"So, I guess there's been a war here, and you lost?"

Arthur did not answer.

"Boy, do you look like shit. You were supposed to come in today, and when you didn't show, I got worried. Looks like I was right, huh?"

Again, Arthur did not answer.

"Okay, they tortured you, they severed your vocal chords. Yoo-hoo, say something, are you deaf? It's me, your partner! Are you catatonic or did you tie on such a big one that you're still drunk?"

Paul saw that Arthur had begun to sob. He sat down beside him and put his arm around his shoulder.

"Arthur, what's going on?"

"She's dead, she died. She began to disappear, just like that. They killed her. I can't get over it, Paul. I can't."

"I can see that." Paul took Arthur in his arms and held him tight. "Go on, cry, buddy, cry, cry all you want. They say the tears help wash away the pain."

"But that's all I've been doing!"

"Well, keep right on going. Look's as if there's more where that came from."

Paul noticed the phone lying with the receiver off the cradle. He got up and replaced it.

"I've called you two hundred times, but it didn't occur to you to put the phone back on the hook!"

"Screw the phone, Paul!"

"You have to snap out of this, pal. You know, this whole business with the ghost was too much. It went too far, and now it looks as if it's going too far even for you. It was a dream, Arthur. You had a crazy ride. Now you have to come back to reality, get your feet back on the ground. You fell in love with a woman in a coma, then you invented a story about her being with you, you stole her body—it was all pure hallucination. And now you're in mourning for a ghost. Do you realize that there's a shrink in this city who's a billionaire and doesn't yet know it! You need help, my friend. You have no choice: I'm not leaving you like this. This whole thing was only a dream that turned into a nightmare."

Paul was interrupted by the sound of the phone ringing. He picked it up, then handed it to Arthur.

"It's some cop. He's pissed as hell! Says it's urgent."

"I have nothing to say to anyone."

Paul put his hand over the mouthpiece. "Speak to him or I'll shove the phone down your throat." He pressed the phone to Arthur's ear. Arthur listened, then jumped to his feet. He thanked Pilger for calling, then began searching frantically for his keys.

"Mind telling me what's going on?" Paul asked.

"No time, got to find my keys."

"Are they coming to arrest you?"

"No! Quit talking crap and help me find my keys!"

"You must be feeling better if you're starting to mouth off at me."

Arthur found his keys, apologized to Paul, told him he had no time to explain but that he would call him that night.

Paul raised an eyebrow. "I don't know where you're heading, but if you're going to be seen in public, I suggest you change clothes and splash some water on your face."

Arthur glanced at his reflection in the living room mirror and dashed into the bathroom. In a few minutes he was washed, shaved, and changed. He raced down the stairs to the garage without even saying good-bye.

After crossing the city as fast as he could, Arthur parked his car at San Francisco Memorial Hospital. Not bothering to lock the car doors, he raced into the reception area, then to the fifth floor.

Mrs. Kline was sitting on a chair just outside Lauren's room. As soon as she saw him, she rose to meet him. She put her arms around him and kissed him on the cheek.

"I don't know you, we only met that one time down on the Marina. But the dog recognized you. I don't understand why, I don't understand everything, but I do know that, for whatever reason and however it came about, what you did prevented me from letting her die and I owe you so much that I'll never know how to thank you."

Then she filled in the details Pilger had omitted on the phone. Lauren had emerged from her coma last Friday. Suddenly, she began to move her fingers and hands. Since last night she had been keeping her eyes open for hours on end, scrutinizing everything going on around her. But she was still unable to speak—all those weeks with a feeding tube had severely compromised her vocal cords, and it would take time for them to heal. And this morning she had responded to a question with the batting of an eyelid. She was weak and the mere raising of her arm seemed to require tremendous effort. This the doctors attributed to muscle atrophy, due to prolonged immobility. That too, with time and therapy, could be dealt with. And finally, her brain scan and MRI were promising.

Arthur smiled and hugged Mrs. Kline.

Arthur went into the room without hearing the rest of the report. The cardiac monitor was emitting a regular and reassuring beep. Lauren was sleeping with her eyes closed. Her skin was still pale, but her beauty was unchanged. He was overcome by emotion when he saw her. He sat down beside the bed and, taking her hand in his, kissed the curve of her palm. Then he settled into a chair and remained there all night, for hours, watching her.

The next morning, she opened her eyes, looked at him intently, and smiled.

"Everything's fine, I'm here," he said softly. "Don't tire yourself, you'll be talking soon."

She frowned, hesitated, gave him another smile, then fell back to sleep.

Epilogue

ARTHUR RETURNED TO THE HOSPITAL EVERY DAY. HE spoke to Lauren constantly, telling her what was happening in the outside world. She could not speak, but she always stared at him while he spoke to her. Only her eyes had changed—their color had become less turbulent, less indistinct, less like a newborn's.

Arthur and Mrs. Kline took turns: one or the other was with Lauren at all times. One day, as Arthur was arriving, Mrs. Kline came out of Lauren's room into the hall to give him the news. That morning, Lauren had recovered the power of speech. She had spoken a few words in a hoarse, rasping voice.

Arthur went in and sat down beside her. She was sleeping. He ran his hand over her hair and softly stroked her forehead, whispering, "How I've missed the sound of your voice."

She opened her eyes and placed her hand on his. She

looked at him with wondering eyes as she asked, "Who are you? Why are you here every day?"

Arthur instantly understood. His heart skipped a beat. Then he smiled with great tenderness and love and replied:

"What I have to tell you is not easy to understand, impossible to accept. But if you will listen to our story—if you are willing to trust me—then maybe in the end you'll believe me. And it's very important that you, in particular, should believe me. For without knowing it, you are the only person in the world I can share our secret with."

Acknowledgments

Nathalie Andre, Paul Boujenah, Kamel Berkane, Bernard Fixot, Philippe Guez,, Rebecca Hayat, Raymond and Daniele Levy, Lorraine Levy, Remi Mangin, Coco Miller, Manon Sbaiz and Aline Souliers
and
Bernard Berrault, Greer Kessel Hendricks and Susanna Lea.